P9-CBK-639

Out of Control . . .

Lucas poured some of the amber liquid into each shot glass and handed one to me. "No thanks," I said, feeling way too wild already. "You have mine."

"Okay. Cheers," he said, drinking them both down.

I bounced my leg to the beat of the music, then grabbed his hand and said, "Let's dance!"

I don't remember when Lucas shut off the lights. Or when he pulled me down on the couch and we started kissing. But suddenly the lights went on again. I blinked and jerked away from Lucas. What was I doing?

Matt stood at the front of the stairs, staring at Lucas and me, our coats in his hands. He hurled my coat to the floor, turned around and slammed the door behind him.

"Matt!" I grabbed my coat and dashed after him up the stairs. "Matt, wait! Please," I wailed. "Please let me explain."

He whirled around, his face distorted in fury. "What's to explain? I come with my girl to a party. She goes downstairs and makes out with another guy. You make me sick!"

"But Matt! I wasn't—"

He cut me off. "You really are crazy, Karen, aren't you?"

Books in the REAL LIFE Series

OBSESSED
CALL ME CATHY
MY BEST FRIEND DIED
HELP ME

Available from ARCHWAY Paperbacks

For orders other than by individual consumers, Archway Books grants a discount on the purchase of **10 or more** copies of single titles for special markets or premium use. For further details, please write to the Vice-President of Special Markets, Pocket Books, 1230 Avenue of the Americas, New York, NY 10020.

For information on how individual consumers can place orders, please write to Mail Order Department, Paramount Publishing, 200 Old Tappan Road, Old Tappan, NJ 07675.

REAL LIFE

Help Me!

Wendy Corsi Staub

AN ARCHWAY PAPERBACK
Published by POCKET BOOKS
New York   London   Toronto   Sydney   Tokyo   Singapore

The sale of this book without its cover is unauthorized. If you purchased this book without a cover, you should be aware that it was reported to the publisher as "unsold and destroyed." Neither the author nor the publisher has received payment for the sale of this "stripped book."

This book is a work of fiction. Although suggested in part by certain actual events, persons and circumstances, *Real Life: Help Me* is not a factual account. Numerous incidents, details and other plot devices have been created for dramatic effect. Names, characters and places in this story are fictitious or are used in a fictitious manner. Any similarity to real persons, living or dead, is not intended.

AN ARCHWAY PAPERBACK *Original*

 An Archway Paperback published by
POCKET BOOKS, a division of Simon & Schuster Inc.
1230 Avenue of the Americas, New York, NY 10020

Copyright © 1995 by Parachute Press, Inc.

All rights reserved, including the right to reproduce this book or portions thereof in any form whatsoever. For information address Pocket Books, 1230 Avenue of the Americas, New York, NY 10020

ISBN: 0-671-87274-5

First Archway Paperback printing May 1995

10 9 8 7 6 5 4 3 2

AN ARCHWAY PAPERBACK and colophon are registered trademarks of Simon & Schuster Inc.

Cover photo by Franco Accornero

Printed in the U.S.A.

IL 7+

It Happened to Me . . .
It Could Happen to You.

REAL LIFE books are inspired by the lives of people who want to share their stories with you. The books re-create important events that offered these teens many choices, many chances and many changes. Although the actual names, places and incidents are fictional, the characters in these books have lives just like yours, feelings just like yours, and stories that could be yours!

For my mother-in-law, Claire Staub,
and my father-in-law, Leonard Staub,
with love.

And for my husband, Mark,
as always.

With special thanks to my aunt, Marian E. Corsi,
for all your valuable assistance
with my research.

Elena Ogrin?
November, 1995

Help Me

1

Wednesday, December 8

Gina"—I cut her off in midsentence—"that's ridiculous."

She widened her dark brown eyes at me and shook her head so that her springy curls bobbed back and forth against her shoulders. "It is not. It says so right here," she insisted, her breath coming out in frosty puffs. She pointed a mittened hand at a paperback on top of the stack of schoolbooks she was lugging home.

I grabbed the book. The title was *Written in the Stars: Finding Your Astrological Mate.*

"Oh, sure. It says in this book that Gina Petrillo and Teddy Kozlowski were destined to go to the Valley

Cove High School Winter Gala together on— What's Saturday?"

"December eleventh. But the book doesn't say anything like *that*. It says that Scorpios—which I am—and Cancers—which Teddy is—are the strongest and most spiritually linked pair in the whole zodiac. Here, I'll show you." She took the book back and started flipping through the pages like crazy.

"That's all right, Gina, I don't need to see." Shaking my head, I started walking again.

She'd been thrilled ever since he invited her. Gina had had only three or four dates in her entire life, which is pretty few, considering that we're almost halfway through our sophomore year at Valley Cove High. It was hard to understand why. She was really cute and really nice. I guess she was a little shy, though. She was always telling me that if she were tall like me, and had my hair, her troubles would be over. Yeah, right. Like I didn't have any troubles!

"And," Gina was saying, "listen to this: 'Scorpio women are loyal, passionate, and ambitious'—that's me."

"True," I replied absently. My thoughts wandered to the dance on Saturday. "Matt asked me in biology lab today what color I'm wearing. I wonder what kind of corsage he's getting me."

"Teddy hasn't asked me about my dress." She looked worried.

"He will."

2

"I still can't believe he asked me. And I can't believe Matt Upshaw asked you, either."

"What's that supposed to mean?"

"Relax, Karen. All I mean is that after you guys had that big blowup in September, I didn't think he'd ask you out again."

"Yeah, well, it took him almost three months, and it's not like we weren't speaking to each other the whole time. I mean, you can't not speak to someone who's your assigned lab partner in biology, even if you are mad at him. Matt tried to give me the silent treatment for a few weeks, but—"

"Can you blame him? You know Matt's shy. It probably took him, like, a month to work up the nerve to ask you out the first time. And then you—"

"So what are you going to get Teddy for Christmas?" I cut in, to change the subject.

"Huh?"

"There's not much time to waste. Only sixteen shopping days left, right?"

"I guess, but—you think I should get him something?"

"Uh, I thought you told me you were going to."

"I never said that. But you think I should?"

"If *you* think you should. I mean, not some big, significant boyfriend-girlfriend gift, but maybe some little token."

"Some little token?" Gina said anxiously. "You mean like a tree ornament or something?"

"Nah. On second thought, forget it. It's too soon to get him a present. You might scare him off."

"That's what I thought." Gina grabbed my arm.

"Hey!" I said. "I was just—"

"You were just about to get run over, Karen. Sometimes I worry about what's going to happen to you if I'm not around."

"Gina, you're not my guardian angel."

"No, I'm only your best friend, and I'd like to keep you around."

I'd lived next door to Gina since we were six, and even then she was the motherly type. Maybe it was because she was the oldest kid in a big family. Or maybe it was because she'd inherited her mother's motherly genes. Mrs. Petrillo was a little round Italian lady who was always stirring a big pot of marinara sauce.

Ever since I was little, I've secretly wished my mom were more like her. But you wouldn't catch Sheila Spencer cooking spaghetti unless she'd gone into her cooking mood and made, like, five pots of it, along with trays of lasagna and ziti and loaves of garlic bread. When she decides to do anything, she tends to go overboard.

Lately she's been acting more and more loony. She goes ballistic about a new project, talking about it day and night and going crazy with plans.

Like, a few weeks ago she decided we needed a bigger deck on the back of our house so we can do more entertaining this summer. She wanted to fix up the backyard, too, with herb gardens and a flagstone path. She was obsessed with it, calling landscapers and making plans. But then one day she just dropped the whole idea.

That was when she slipped back into what I'm starting to think of as her other self—the one who's basically quiet and spends a lot of time watching television and sleeping. Sometimes she even cries for no reason that I can see. But it's almost a relief when she goes through her down times, because she doesn't bug me or my brother, Ethan, or my dad. In fact, she hardly talks at all. I guess those times are better than the ones when her motor is running on high, because you never know when she'll pick a fight and then get hysterical. Sometimes she'll start throwing things, and my brother and I will get out of the house as fast as we can. If it's late at night I'll bury my head in my pillows. I try to black out as much as I can.

"Okay, right here," Gina interrupted my thoughts, pointing to a paragraph in her book. " 'No one understands the Cancer man's need for nurturing better than the Scorpio woman, who—' "

"Gina, I am not interested in this zodiac stuff, okay? When are you going to drop it?"

I knew that was mean, but I couldn't help myself. Sometimes it's like I have no control over what comes out of my mouth.

Before she could respond, I tacked on a quick, "Sorry."

Gina just shrugged. "You know, Karen, I think I

know why you're such a moody person. You're a Taurus."

I stopped in the middle of a yawn. "Moody?"

"Tauruses are prone to mood swings."

"I don't have mood swings!"

"Sure you do. Just a few Saturdays ago you were so depressed you couldn't even get out of bed!"

I never should have told her about that. But I had to tell her something—we had plans to go to a football game that day and I backed out on her. One minute I was okay. And then the next I was so overcome by this terrible, bleak feeling, like I was paralyzed. It came out of nowhere, and I couldn't shake it. All I did the entire day—and the next day, too—was cry or stare off into space. Afterward I decided it must have been some kind of hormonal thing, because it wasn't the first time it had happened to me. It was just the first time I told anyone about it. And obviously, that was my first mistake.

My second mistake was showing a poem I'd written while I was in that weird mood to Howard Pepper, the editor of our school literary magazine. After he scanned it he gave me a probing look, then read the first three lines back to me. I still remember them clearly.

> Pain chokes my soul like bile, it
> mangles my bitter heart until it
> oozes crimson on cold concrete . . .

"Look, Gina," I said, shoving the poem and Howard out of my head, "everyone gets bummed once in a while, not just Tauruses. I mean, look at my mother! She's always up and down. She's the moodiest person I know."

"When's her birthday?"

"January twentieth."

"Hmmm." She consulted her book. "She's a Capricorn, but on the cusp with Aquarius. I'm not sure what that means."

"I don't *care* what that means, Gina!"

"See? You're in a bad mood right now."

"I am not." We stopped in front of the Petrillos' house. "So call me later," I told Gina.

"If I have time. We're eating dinner early tonight so we can go to some Christmas choir program at St. Bernadette's."

That was the elementary school her brothers and sisters attended. Gina went there, too, but only up to ninth grade. Since her parents couldn't afford to send her to St. Isabel's High School in Providence, she transferred to Valley Cove High to start tenth grade this past September. I was really psyched about that. Even though we've been best friends forever, we'd never gone to the same school.

"I'm freezing," Gina said, stamping her boots on the sidewalk. "I'm going in. See you later."

"See you— Hey, wait," I called, remembering something. I dug through my bag, looking for the wrapped box I'd put there that morning. "Here," I said at last, handing it to Gina.

"What's this?"

"It's a present."

"But Karen, I thought we weren't going to exchange gifts until Christmas Eve."

"It's not a Christmas gift. It's just something I saw and wanted you to have." I nudged her, anxious for her reaction when she saw it. "Go ahead, open it."

Bouncing a little in excitement, she started undoing the paper, careful not to rip it. It was a really pretty floral print I'd bought especially for her. Gina was crazy about anything floral. You should see her bedroom. She got the paper off and opened the small box. She squealed when she saw what was inside. "Oh, Karen, it's beautiful!"

"You can wear it to the dance," I told her as she lifted out the antique rhinestone pin and examined it more closely. "It goes with your dress—the perfect finishing touch."

"It is! I love it. Thanks, Karen—you're such a great friend."

I gave her a big hug. "So are you."

"I can't wait to try it on my dress. I think the stones are the exact same color pink."

"Let me know how it looks."

"I will. Thanks again. I love it!" Gina waved as she ran up her driveway.

I walked the few yards to our mailbox and opened it. It was empty. Which was unusual, since my mother was an obsessive mail-order shopper. She was on practically every mailing list in the country, and she got a ton of junk mail every day.

I shrugged and closed the box. Maybe we hadn't gotten anything today. Or maybe—as much as I hoped it wasn't true—my mother had already taken the mail inside. And that had better not be what happened, because she was supposed to be at work. But I saw that the kitchen light was on as I walked up the back steps and across the deck. And when I opened the door, there she was.

"Mom, what are you doing home?" I asked, starting into the kitchen.

I stopped short, my hand still on the knob, and gaped. She was on her hands and knees in front of the open refrigerator, wearing my father's old flannel pajamas and these stupid slippers she got from my brother Ethan last Christmas—they were red and furry and had Santa heads on the toes. Her hair hadn't been combed all day.

But it wasn't just what she looked like—it was what the kitchen looked like.

Everything that had been in the refrigerator was now spread out all over the floor. There were bowls of leftovers, jars of condiments, cartons of juice, and bags of produce. A jar was lying on its side, the lid obviously not on tightly enough. Something sticky and purple was oozing out all over the tiles around it. Most of the cupboard doors were open, as if she'd been cleaning them out and stopped halfway through to tackle the refrigerator. The kitchen reeked of bleach and something rotten—like leftovers that had gone bad.

"Karen, close the door! You're letting all the heat out," my mother said, dipping a sponge into a bucket and then, without wringing it out, slapping it against a wire shelf. Water went flying everywhere, but it didn't even faze her.

I closed the door behind me and started picking my way across the room. "Mom," I said, wrinkling my nose, "what stinks?"

"I don't know—that's why I'm cleaning out the fridge. I opened the door this afternoon to get some orange juice, and *whew!*"

I sighed and shook my head. "What are you doing home, anyway?"

She had just started a new job a few weeks ago as a secretary at an insurance agency in Providence. Her friend Amy had to pull strings to get her hired, since my mother didn't have the best references in the world. She'd been fired from two secretarial jobs in the past two years. Actually she claimed that she quit the second time, but I knew she was probably lying. She called in sick constantly, and when she did manage to go in, she was late.

"Aren't you supposed to be at work, Mom?" I asked again when she didn't answer me.

She stopped scrubbing, but didn't turn around. "I had a terrible headache this morning, Karen. I called in sick."

"Mom—"

"Karen, I'm the adult around here, remember?"

I knew I should just shut up, but I couldn't. "Well, if you're so sick, why are you in here cleaning? Why aren't you in bed?"

"I felt better after I spent the morning lying down. And I took some aspirin. Then I decided, why waste a whole day in bed?"

I rolled my eyes and stepped over a cellophane-covered bowl of wilted salad from the night before. I was halfway into the dining room when my mother called, "Karen?"

"What?" I asked impatiently.

"Don't tell Daddy I didn't go to work today. I don't want him to worry. You know how he worries when I'm sick."

He worries when you play hooky *because he needs you to work so he can pay the bills you rack up on the Visa card! He worries because you've had this job for two weeks and this is the second time you've called in sick and he doesn't want you getting fired again! He worries because you've always been a little nutty, but lately you've been acting crazy!*

I was screaming at her inside my head, but out loud all I said was, "Yeah. Fine. I won't tell Dad."

2

Thursday, December 9

When I got home from school on Thursday, my mother was at it again in the kitchen, cleaning. When she launched into a big explanation about why she hadn't gone to work, I cut her off, saying, "Any mail for me?"

"An airmail letter. It's on the hall table."

It had to be from Sophia. She was my pen pal who lived in Italy, and it had been over two months since I'd heard from her. I wondered if she'd received the Christmas gift I'd mailed her right after Thanksgiving. I'd been in a holiday frenzy that week.

I made all my Christmas cards and mailed them

that same week. I love to paint and draw, so I created a different holiday scene for each card with ink and watercolors. All my friends loved them, and so did Mrs. Rosenbaum, my favorite teacher. She's Jewish, so I made a Hanukkah scene for her. I had to look up pictures of menorahs at the library so my menorah would be accurate. She told me she couldn't get over how much time I'd spent on her card.

I picked up the letter, went up the stairs, and paused in front of Ethan's closed door.

My brother was basically an introvert, spending most of his time either shooting baskets alone on the driveway or blasting rap music from the stereo in his room. We didn't talk to each other much, but sometimes I went into his room and read or sketched while he listened to music. We were used to hanging out together without talking.

Since everything was quiet behind the door, I knew he mustn't be home yet, but I knocked anyway. "Eth?"

No answer.

From the kitchen I heard a loud clattering sound, like an entire rack of pots and pans had just fallen onto the floor.

Shaking my head, I went into my room and slammed the door. Then I found my Soul Asylum tape and played "Runaway Train" as loud as I could on my Walkman.

* * *

I ran around the corner onto Sunset Lane and fought the temptation to stop jogging and walk the rest of the way home. It was well past dusk now, and my ears were freezing. But I forced myself to keep up a steady pace. I could see our house ahead, and I made myself keep jogging until the end of our driveway.

But it wasn't like I was running to lose weight or anything. Luckily, I'm tall—five feet seven—and my weight pretty much hovers around a hundred and thirty. No, I had gone running to burn off energy, because I was going stir-crazy in my room. After reading the letter from Sophia, I'd written her a ten-page one, filling her in on what had been going on in my love life. I told her all about Matt and the dance. I couldn't remember if I'd written to her about what happened between Matt and me back in September, so I told her that, too.

First, though, I backtracked and told her how I'd had a crush on him since the first day of school last year, when I was a freshman. And even though we both worked on the school literary magazine together, we never really talked much. Matt was too shy to start a conversation.

But then, when school started sophomore year, this past September, we ended up as biology lab partners because the teacher matched everyone alphabetically, and *Upshaw* followed *Spencer*. We gradually started talking and found out we had more in common than the literary magazine. We both loved to rent old Brat

Pack eighties movies, like *St. Elmo's Fire* and *The Breakfast Club*. We were both crazy about sushi, "Melrose Place," and the Lemonheads. And Matt knew Ethan—it turned out his father had coached my brother's Little League team a few years back. So we had a lot to talk about. Then Matt asked me to go to the homecoming dance with him.

I was really excited about it. I got a new dress and shoes and everything. But then, the Friday before the dance, something happened.

I didn't tell Sophia exactly what it was. How could I tell anyone the truth—that I'd completely fallen apart for some reason? That when I woke up on Friday I couldn't drag myself out of bed? It was so strange—just like the time when I was supposed to go to the football game with Gina. I was just completely depressed. I couldn't eat, or talk, or do anything but cry or stare at the ceiling.

It lasted for a few days. I ended up calling Matt on Saturday, only an hour before he was supposed to pick me up, to tell him I couldn't go to the dance. At first he was totally silent. I don't think he believed me when I said I was sick. Then he kept telling me I sounded bad—like something else was wrong. And I finally hung up on him because I couldn't deal with his questions.

After that we didn't talk much, even though we still saw each other every day in school. I did my best to make it up to him—to be friendly and nice whenever we were together. Luckily Matt warmed up to me again, and when he got up the nerve to ask me to the Christmas dance, I was flying high.

In my letter, I told Sophia about the dance on Saturday night, and how I would finally get to wear the dress I'd bought for homecoming.

I mailed the letter to Sophia when I'd jogged by the mailbox a little while ago. Now I picked up my speed and sprinted the rest of the way to our driveway.

My dad's car wasn't there. He must be working late again. I sighed as I walked around to the back and climbed the steps to the deck. Dad hardly ever made it home for dinner these days. In fact, lots of times he didn't get in until after I'd gone to bed. I'd know he came home because I'd hear him arguing with my mom. Usually it was about money or something she'd promised and forgotten to do, like drop his shirts off to be laundered or make a deposit at the bank.

When I walked into the kitchen, I found my mom and Ethan sitting at the table. The small portable television in the corner was blaring, and Mom was just opening a pizza box.

"You're just in time, Karen," she said, ripping off the box top and tossing it over her shoulder onto the floor.

"Yeah, something new for dinner—pizza," Ethan said sarcastically. He helped himself to two large pieces, anyway, and then stood up.

"Where do you think you're going?" my mother asked.

"To eat in my room."

"No you're not. We're going to sit here and eat dinner like a family. Karen, sit down."

I kicked off my sneakers, padded over to the table, and slid into my usual seat.

A family dinner.

What a joke.

Takeout pizza, as usual, the TV on, as usual, and dear old Dad missing in action, as usual. I couldn't remember the last time Mom cooked a meal—or Dad had been home to eat with us.

The Petrillos all sat down together every single night in their dining room. They ate these fantastic home-cooked meals, like meat loaf or pork chops. They weren't allowed to have the television on, either. Mr. Petrillo insisted that they have a conversation.

I grabbed a slice of pizza even though I wasn't hungry, plunked it on the paper plate my mother had set at my place, and reached for a can of Pepsi from the six-pack in the center of the table.

"Can you move your head, Kar?" my brother asked, trying to see the television screen.

"Sorry." I sat back and glanced at the set. He was watching some sports program on ESPN. Boring.

"So," Mom said around a mouthful of cheese, "are you excited about the dance, Karen?"

"Yeah. It's going to be great."

"Do you have stockings to wear? I'm going to run out to the drugstore tomorrow, and I can pick some up for you."

"No, thanks, I'm all set."

"I remember a Christmas dance I went to when I was in high school," she said.

Just then the phone rang. My mother answered it, and it was one of her friends. She got involved in a long conversation, and her pizza grew cold.

I finished my slice and went into my room again, looking around for something to do. I was too restless to draw. I put Sophia's letter into the shoebox on the shelf of my closet, the one marked "Cards and Letters." It was almost full. I snapped a rubber band around it to keep the top on, then found an empty box under my bed and labeled it. I put it on my shelf, careful to line it up with the other boxes. I scanned them absently, making sure they were in the right order: "Magazine Clippings," "Photo Negatives," "Receipts," "Travel Brochures."

I pulled the last one down. I hadn't browsed through it in a long time. I used to send for brochures of different places that I'd eventually like to visit. I hadn't done it in a while, though.

I sat on my bed and flipped through the contents of the box. All the places were so—ordinary. I mean, Disney World? What had I been thinking? If I went anywhere now, I'd want it to be someplace exotic. Like Europe. In fact, I could always visit Sophia. She'd probably love to have me come and stay with her.

Well, why not? I asked myself, sitting back on the

floor and thinking about it. I mean, why couldn't I go to Italy?

I wondered how much it would cost. Usually I made money by baby-sitting, but recently the Talbots, who have three kids, had decided their son Jason, who was almost twelve, was old enough to watch his brother and sister. And the Murdocks, my other regular customers, had moved away in October. So I couldn't count on baby-sitting anymore. I was too old for that, anyway. I needed a real job. If I got one now, I could save up enough money to go to Italy by the summer.

I jumped up and went over to my desk. I found my calculator and a notebook and spent the next several hours in a frenzy, making phone calls and lists. I called every airline in the phone book and compared their fares. Then I created a savings plan, based on a part-time job at seventy-five dollars a week. I even started to make a list of what I would need to pack, but I had to interrupt that to go look up Italy in the almanac to see what the weather was like in Naples in August.

The books were downstairs in the family room. I thought I might find my mother on the couch watching TV, but she wasn't there. The house was quiet, and I remembered both my parents' bedroom door and Ethan's were closed. I grabbed a can of Pepsi on the way back up to my room. I wanted to tell someone about my trip, so I decided to call Gina.

I punched out the Petrillos' number and waited. It

rang four times, which was odd—usually someone snatched it up immediately.

"Hello?" That was Gina's father. He didn't sound like his usual cheery self, though.

"Hi, Mr. Petrillo. It's Karen. Is Gina there?" I asked in a rush.

"She's in bed," he said—grumpily, I thought.

"She's in *bed?*"

"Yes. Karen, it's past midnight. Why are you calling so late?"

"It's past *midnight?*" I echoed again. "You're kidding."

"I'm not kidding."

"Oh, well, sorry. I'll talk to her tomorrow."

"Fine." He banged down the phone without saying goodbye. God, what was up with him? You'd think I'd done something illegal.

3

_____   _____

Friday, December 10

On the way to school I told Gina about my plans to go to Italy and begged her to come with me.

She kept telling me to stop talking so fast because she could barely understand me.

"I'm just really excited, Gina."

"But where would we get the money? A trip like that would cost thousands of dollars, Karen!"

"Not *thousands*. Hundreds. Okay, maybe *a* thousand. And anyway, that's the other part of my perfect plan. We could get jobs! Look," I said, and pulled the classified section out of my bag.

"What's that?" Gina asked, stopping on the sidewalk and taking it from me.

"See? I circled all the places that are looking for part-time help. There are tons of jobs out there."

"Yeah, but Karen, these aren't all—I mean, why'd you circle this one? It says 'Mature Woman Wanted.'"

"So? I'm mature."

"Yeah, but I think they mean like a grandmother or something. This job is child care—taking care of an infant every afternoon."

"So? All they need is a baby-sitter. I've got plenty of experience with that, and so do you."

"Yeah, but—oh, never mind." She handed the classified section back to me. "Good luck."

"Oh, come on, Gina. Aren't you going to do this with me?"

"Karen, where do you come up with these crazy plans? We can't just go off to Italy. What about school?"

"We'd go during summer vacation. I've got the whole thing figured out. Come over after school, and I'll show you all my notes and stuff."

"My parents would never let me go to Italy alone."

"You won't be alone. Tell them you're going with me. Come on, Gina. Live a little," I said impatiently as we rounded the corner and the redbrick Valley Cove High School came into view. "Your parents will let you. They *have* to."

"Yeah, well, my dad was kind of upset with you this morning. He said you called me in the middle of the night."

I waved my hand casually. "It wasn't exactly the 'middle of the night.'"

"I don't know about you, Karen," Gina continued. "You've been acting weird lately. I never know what you're going to do next."

I said, pointing, "Hey, isn't that Teddy over there?"

She squinted at the boy in the blue jacket who was crossing the sidewalk half a block ahead. "Is it?"

"Yeah, I think so."

Her hands flew up to pat her springy black curls. "Do I look all right?" she asked anxiously.

"You look terrific."

"But my hair came out so frizzy today."

"No, it didn't, Gina. I *love* your hair." Which was the truth. Mine was plain light brown, parted in the middle, the wavy kind that never does what you want it to. I had finally managed to grow it past my shoulders and vowed never to cut it short again.

"Come on," Gina said, grabbing my arm. "Let's hurry and catch up to Teddy."

The first thing I did when I got home that afternoon was answer a bunch of ads I had circled in the paper. When I called, most of them told me to come in and fill out applications. A few—like the people looking for a "mature woman"—told me to forget it.

But one place, a clothing store in Barrington, which is a few towns over, told me to come in the next morning for an interview. I think they were impressed

23

when I mentioned that I was into fashion design. Which was true. I had notebooks full of designs.

In fact, I was hoping to go to the Fashion Institute of Technology in New York City for college. My parents pointed out that R.I.S.D.—Rhode Island School of Design—was closer, and I could live at home if I went there. But I had my mind set on F.I.T.

As soon as I hung up with the manager of the clothing store, I heard a door slam. My mother was home from work. As she started up the stairs, I ran over to my bedroom door, opened it, and called, "Hey, Mom?"

She came walking down the hall, acting distracted. "Yeah?" she asked, glancing at me.

"Can you give me a ride to Barrington tomorrow morning?"

"Why do you have to go there?" she asked, pausing in the doorway.

"I have a job interview at that new clothing store near the Newport Creamery," I said. I wasn't about to go into the whole thing about the trip to Italy. I'd tell her later, when I started working and saving money.

"A job interview? That's great. Sure, I'll drive you."

"Thanks. It's at ten, so we should leave here by nine-thirty to make sure I get there on time."

"Karen, it's a fifteen-minute drive."

"Come on, Mom—what if there's traffic?"

She raised an eyebrow. "Around here?"

"Please, Mom? This is really important to me."

"Okay," she said, and gave a little wave. "I have to

get ready. Daddy's coming home early tonight, and he's taking me to the Lobster Pot for dinner."

"Have fun," I called after her.

I was way too keyed up about everything—the dance, the interview, Italy—to sleep. I sat at my desk, furiously sketching clothing designs in my pad. I created a whole line of travel clothes that had an Italian flair and decided they were good enough to be professional.

When I turned off the light and climbed into bed, I was still thinking about the sketches. Maybe I'd send them to Calvin Klein or someone. I imagined him snatching them up and demanding to meet me. He would fly me to New York, and soon I'd become the most famous young designer in the world.

After a while I decided that it was time I got to sleep.

But I couldn't stop my thoughts from racing.

The longer I lay in bed—telling myself that if I didn't drift off soon I'd have huge dark circles under my eyes for my date with Matt—the more restless I became.

Finally, at around two in the morning, I turned on the light again and went over to my bookshelf for something to read. I had dozens of books, everything from *Are You My Mother?*, which was my favorite Dr. Seuss story, to every novel Mary Higgins Clarke had ever written. But I'd read everything on that shelf a million times.

Frustrated, I decided to go find my new copy of *Sassy* magazine. I carefully opened my door so it wouldn't creak, then padded along the short hall and down the steps to the family room.

The lights were off, but even before I got all the way into the room I saw the bluish flickering light from the television. My mother was on her stationary bike in her nightgown, pedaling away and watching TV.

"Hey, what are you doing up?" she asked, still rhythmically pumping the bike, not even breathless.

"I can't sleep."

"Join the club. Why don't you hang out here for a while. This movie just started two minutes ago."

"What is it?"

"Meatballs."

"Really? Ethan and I saw that twice already. I'll only watch until I get sleepy."

But I stayed for the whole movie, and eventually Mom got off her bike and joined me on the couch. She was at one end, I was at the other, and we shared an afghan. There wasn't much room, since we were both built the same—tall with impossibly long legs.

Finally the credits rolled, and I thought maybe I could go upstairs and fall asleep. My mother was dozing off, and I nudged her under the afghan. When she opened her eyes, I said, "I'm going to bed. G'night."

"Night."

Halfway up I remembered something and turned around. "Mom?"

"Yeah?" She was back on the bike again, flipping channels with the remote control.

"Um, don't forget about my interview tomorrow morning, okay?"

"What int— Oh, right. What time do you have to be there again?"

"Ten o'clock."

"Okay." She yawned.

I put my foot on the next step and paused again. "Aren't you coming to bed?"

"In a while. Daddy's up there snoring away. Who can sleep with all that noise?"

I shrugged. "Okay. G'night," I said again, and continued on up to bed.

4

Saturday, December 11

As soon as I opened my eyes I knew something was wrong. "Oh, my God," I said out loud, glancing at my clock. It was past nine.

How could that be? Had I forgotten to set the alarm?

I jumped out of bed and dashed for my bedroom door. Throwing it open, I hurried down to the kitchen, which was empty. So was the living room. My father, I knew, would be at the gym. He went there bright and early every Saturday morning to play racquetball with his friend Mr. Kessler.

I ran down the hall, past Ethan's closed door, and saw that the one to my parents' room was open.

"Mom?" I called, bursting in. "Mom, why didn't you wake me?"

There was no answer. I glanced at the rumpled, unmade bed, and at the nightgown she'd been wearing the night before, which was tossed over a chair.

She must be down in the family room.

But she wasn't.

The house was empty, and when I looked out at the driveway, I saw something that made my growing anger erupt into rage. Both cars, my father's *and* hers, were gone.

"Ethan?" I shouted, running back toward his room. I banged on the door, but there was no reply. He wasn't home, either.

Starting to cry, I went back into the kitchen to check the wall clock, to make sure something wasn't wrong with mine.

It was nine-fifteen.

I dashed into the bathroom and took a quick shower anyway. And I zipped back into my room and threw on the outfit I'd gotten ready last night.

It was nine-thirty-five by that time.

Panicking, I carelessly blew my hair dry with one hand and put on makeup with the other. As a result, my hair had some stupid-looking dip around the part that I somehow couldn't fix with gel or by wetting it again. And the liner around my eyes, which were still puffy from crying, was crooked. I did my best to fix it with Q-Tips.

And the whole time I was struggling to get ready, I

was muttering under my breath, cursing my mother, calling her everything I could think of. Back in the kitchen again, I laced up my black leather boots.

I looked out the window. A wet snow was falling, but there was no car, and there was no Sheila Spencer, and the clock was ticking away on the wall, three-quarters of the way toward ten. I was shaking with rage, and I dropped the back of an earring I was trying to stick onto its post. I hunted it down, jabbed it onto the earring, and glanced at the clock again.

About twelve minutes to ten.

I ran into the living room and looked out the window, praying that I'd see my mother's car coming down the snowy street.

"Where *is* she?" I muttered for the millionth time, letting the sheer drapes fall back into place.

Desperate, I ran to the phone and punched out the Petrillos' number. Gina didn't have her license, either, but maybe one of her parents could take me to Barrington. There was no answer, though, and I remembered that Gina had said something about going to her grandmother's.

I thought about Mike Lopez, who lived in the house directly behind our yard. He was a friend of mine, and a year older, so he had a license *and* a car. I dialed his number, and his mother answered.

"Hi, Mrs. Lopez. Is Mike around?" I asked in a rush.

"Karen? Is that you? How have you been?"

"Fine—is he there?"

"Mike? No, he isn't. He went over to the school to decorate for the dance tonight. Are you going?" she asked pleasantly, totally oblivious to my frantic state.

"Listen, Mrs. Lopez, I have to go," I said and banged the phone down. I knew she didn't have a license, so there was no way she could drive me.

It was seven minutes till ten o'clock.

I was crying now. I kept swiping at the tears that were probably smearing my makeup all over my face.

I waited a few more minutes. Then, in desperation, I ran to my room, grabbed the ad that had the store's phone number on it, and called.

"Hello?" I said to the person who answered. I tried to sound calm and professional. "May I please speak to Darlene Curry?"

"Speaking."

"Um, hi, Darlene—" Or should I be calling her "Miss Curry"? "This is Karen Spencer. I was supposed to be at an interview with you this morning—actually, in a few minutes, at ten o'clock."

"Yes?" She didn't sound very friendly. In fact, she sounded cold. Maybe I should have called her "Miss Curry." "And?"

"And, um, I'm running a little late. So I was wondering if we could reschedule for later—maybe this afternoon?"

"I'm sorry, I can't do that."

"But—"

"I've got back-to-back interviews scheduled all day. Anyway, I don't think this would have worked out for

31

you. Punctuality is very important to us. Have a nice day."

She hung up!

"Have a nice *day?*" I repeated incredulously. "Have a nice *day?*"

Just then I heard it. A car pulling into the driveway.

For a moment I just stood there debating whether I should march outside and tell my mom what I thought of her. Or should I wait until she came inside and then tell her?

I waited in the kitchen, arms folded. I heard a door slam, then the trunk lid slam, and then footsteps crunching up the snowy steps and across the deck.

At that moment I considered running over and locking the door so she couldn't get in. I didn't want her near me.

But that was stupid and childish.

And besides, she had keys.

She opened the door, stepped inside, and looked at me. "What are you doing?"

"What are *you* doing?" I asked and snapped into action. I stomped over and stood right in front of her, my hands on my hips as I leaned forward and hollered into her face, "Where have you been? You promised that you'd take me to my interview. You *promised.*"

For a moment she looked blank. I couldn't believe it. She had forgotten all about it! Then I saw a flicker of recognition and something else—regret? But instead of apologizing, she only said, "Well, here I am. Let's go."

"It's ten o'clock. I was supposed to be there at ten."

"So you're a few minutes late." She shrugged and carried the bags over to the counter, put them down, and went back for the ones still on the deck. "Get your coat on and let's go."

"A few minutes late? Where do you think you were taking me, to the movies? This was an *interview!* I can't just show up late!"

"Stop shouting, Karen. I'm sure they'll understand. There's a lot of snow out there. The roads aren't the greatest, and—"

"They will not understand. I already called them, and they told me to forget it!"

She didn't look at me as she closed the door, carried the other two bags over to the counter, and started unloading them.

I just stood there, watching her. She acted calm.

She finished one bag, threw it aside, and started on the next one.

After another moment I said, "You're not even going to apologize?"

"Apologize?" She gave a bitter little laugh. "Fine. You want an apology, Karen? I'm sorry. I'm sorry I offered to drive your brother over to the school instead of making him walk through this miserable weather."

She tossed a loaf of Wonder bread onto the counter then plunked a can of tomato juice on top of it, smushing it. "And I'm sorry I had to stop at the store to get food and some ibuprofen for my goddamn

33

headache. And I'm sorry that the store was jammed and it took me a half hour to get through a line, and I'm sorry that the roads were slippery, and I'm sorry that I didn't risk my life and drive faster so that I could be here to chauffeur you around town!"

With that, she took the last item out of the bag—a jar of pickles—and threw it across the room. Not at me. At the wall. There was a thud and then the jar was on the floor, cracked and spilling pale green juice onto the floor.

I looked at it, then at my mother.

Then I ran up to my room, crying, and slammed the door.

5

I spent the whole day avoiding my mother. At one point, when I was sure she was taking a nap in her room, I sneaked down to the kitchen. I had to figure out a way to get the swelling down around my eyes. First I tried cold wet tea bags, but they didn't do a thing. Then I put ice into a dish towel and went back up to my room. As I was lying on my back, with the ice on my eyes, my mother knocked on the door. Luckily it was locked, because I didn't want to see her. I didn't answer, and finally she went away.

I fell asleep for a while and my eyes were still red and puffy when I woke up. So I put on more eye makeup than I usually wear when I get dressed up—blue liner and peach and blue shadow. And lots of undereye concealer.

I was running late so I got dressed in a rush, still hoping I wouldn't have to face my mother. I heard her come upstairs as I was doing my hair. She stopped in front of my door but didn't knock. As I was putting on my shoes I heard a car pull up. I looked out the window and saw it was Matt's friend Brent's car. Now if I could only get out of the house without having to see my mother.

I rushed down the stairs for my coat. Matt rang the doorbell, and my mother called down, "Is that your date, honey?"

I didn't answer her.

"I'll be right down," she said. "Just let me comb my hair."

My heart was pounding. I don't know what I was so nervous about. Seeing Matt? Facing my mother? Letting Matt see my mother?

All I knew was that I had to get out of the house.

I opened the door, and there was Matt. He looked so different in a suit. Serious and formal. It made me more nervous.

"I'll be right down, Karen!"

"Hi, Matt," I said, pretending I didn't hear her.

"Hi," he said. "I think your mother's calling you."

"Oh—no. She's talking to my brother upstairs."

I put on my coat and Matt tried to help me. It was sort of awkward. I couldn't get one arm in, and Matt laughed a little.

"Ready?" he said.

"Yup," I said and opened the front door.

Just then my mother started down the stairs, calling my name. I pushed Matt in front of me, and he said, "Should we wait for your mother?"

"No," I said, avoiding his eyes.

"But I think she wanted to—"

"Would you just give me a break, Matt?" I said. I didn't want to talk about my mother, see my mother, think about my mother. And I definitely didn't want to explain anything to Matt.

"Sorry," was all he said.

"Let's go," I said.

"Did I tell you how nice you look tonight?" Matt asked in the backseat of the car. We were headed toward Tricia Loomis's house for a party after the dance. Brent had stopped the car for a red light.

"Yup. You told me. But thanks again," I told Matt.

And it was really a sweet thing to say. But now I couldn't help longing for him to *do* something, instead of just talk.

Normally in school Matt seemed too tall and skinny, but tonight he looked broader and more—manly. His dark, wavy hair was the same, though. Short on the sides, a little longer on top. It looked great. And I had been dying to run my fingers through it all night.

I squirmed closer to Matt, wishing he'd put his arm around me or something. But the only time he'd done that all night was when we'd danced. No, he *had* held my hand on the way to the refreshment table once. His grasp was warm and firm, not at all sweaty.

Brent stopped kissing his girlfriend Barbie and muttered something to her, then started driving again.

We pulled up in front of Tricia's house. It was all decorated for Christmas, with green garlands and red bows looped along the white fence in front, a white candle in every window, and a huge wreath on the front door. It looked really pretty in the snow that had been lightly falling all night.

We got out of the car and started up the winding driveway. Matt grabbed my hand to help me pick my way through the snow. I was glad that the driveway was so long. I didn't want to let go of him.

"Careful," he said when I almost slipped. "Here, take my arm instead."

So I did, with both hands. That was better because I could snuggle into his side. He was wearing a really nice dark blue woolen overcoat. I was freezing in my thin coat, which wasn't heavy enough for winter but was dressier than my bulky tweed coat.

When I shivered, Matt said, "Cold?"

"A little."

I imagined him saying huskily, "I'll warm you up," pulling me into his arms and kissing me.

But all he did was smile and say, "Don't worry, we're almost there."

"Yeah," I murmured, bummed.

Inside, music was blasting. People who had seemed stiff and awkward back at the dance were hanging loose. Most of the girls had kicked off their shoes. Lucas Marshall had taken off his tie and wrapped it around his head like a sweatband.

"Pretty wild, huh?" Matt said in my ear.

"Yeah." Reluctantly I let go of his arm.

We took off our coats and he said, "I'll go put these upstairs."

"Okay."

I stood there in the crowded living room, tapping my palms against my thighs to the beat of the music and looking around. I saw a lot of people I knew, including Gina. She was sitting on the piano bench in one corner with Teddy.

I made my way over to them. "Hi," I said, tapping Gina on the shoulder.

She brightened. "Hi!"

"Having fun?"

"Yeah. How about you?"

"Definitely." I hadn't seen much of her at the dance. She and Teddy had been on the floor for one or two slow songs, but the rest of the time I couldn't spot them.

Gina and Teddy seemed pretty cozy. Not wanting to horn in on them, I said, "If you see Matt, tell him I went into the kitchen."

I made my way toward the back of the house. The kitchen was jammed with people. Candace Meyers was there in a tight red strapless dress, her date's tie slung around her neck like a pendant.

"Hey, Karen," she said. *"Love* the black velvet."

"Thanks. Your dress is cool, too."

"Thanks." Candace took a pack of cigarettes out of the little black purse she was carrying and said, "Want one?"

"Why not." I wasn't a smoker, but I was feeling restless and needed something to do. I took one out of her pack, put it between my lips, and leaned forward so she could light it for me. Then she tucked the book of matches back into the cellophane around the pack.

She made a face as soon as she inhaled. "Menthol," she said, making a face again. "I told Jeff to get regulars. Do you like menthol?"

"Sure."

"Here." She shoved the pack at me. "Take them. I'll bum off someone else."

"Thanks," I said, shrugging and tucking the cigarettes into my purse. I probably wouldn't smoke any more. For some reason I didn't think Matt would like it. I made my way back to the living room. Gina and Teddy were gone. I sat on the empty piano bench.

By the time Matt showed up, I'd smoked three cigarettes.

"There you are," he said, appearing in front of me.

"Hi!" I said brightly, sliding over to the edge of the bench. "Want to sit down?"

He did. "I didn't know you smoked," was the first thing he said when he saw me pull out the pack and light one.

"Oh. I don't really." But I took a drag anyway. I really wanted a cigarette. I told myself it would help calm me down. I was feeling pretty edgy by that time. All I wanted to do was be alone with Matt, not surrounded by a crowd.

Matt didn't say anything else about my smoking. In fact, he didn't say much to me at all. He was talking to a kid I barely knew, who was standing on his other side. I started lighting a new cigarette off the old one. I was becoming agitated just sitting there, and I started plotting a way to get Matt upstairs alone.

Then this old U2 song I really like came on. "Hey, they're playing 'With or Without You,'" I told Matt, jumping up and setting my empty cup on the piano keys. "Let's dance!"

He looked annoyed that I had interrupted. "Nah, I don't feel like it," Matt said and resumed his conversation.

I plunked down again, suddenly seething. Why did we have to just sit here on this stupid bench? And why wasn't Matt paying more attention to me?

Agitated, I tapped my foot on the floor.

When Bono started singing, I jumped up and looked at a surprised Matt. "I have to dance," I said abruptly and headed for the dining room, leaving him staring after me.

In the dining room I slipped into the dancing crowd. Normally I wouldn't dance alone like that, but that night I didn't care. I twirled and swung my arms, moving easily and seductively. Maybe Matt would join me if he saw what I was doing.

The next song that came on was some stupid rap

tune that I heard zillions of times last summer. "Oh, *please!*" I shouted at everyone who was dancing to it. "Aren't you guys sick of this song? What a bunch of losers!"

I ignored the looks I was getting—some nasty, some startled—and danced over to the CD player in the corner. There was a CD rack next to it, and I quickly scanned the rows, looking for something I liked. The Lemonheads. Without stopping to think, I jabbed the STOP button.

"Hey!"

"Who did that?"

"Yo, Karen, what are you doing?"

They were such jerks, I thought as I took out the rap CD, tossed it on the floor, and put the Lemonheads on. *Maybe this'll bring Matt the Bore onto the dance floor,* I told myself. I started to dance again. A lot of people were standing around watching me, and some were whispering. Who cared? I was having fun.

The next thing I knew, Lucas Marshall, still wearing his tie around his head, had slipped in front of me. We danced together for the rest of the song.

Then some guy I'd never seen before took the Lemonheads CD off, and I shouted, "What's your problem, loser?"

"What's *your* problem?" he shouted back.

"Hey, you looking for trouble?" Lucas asked, starting toward the guy. "You wanna go outside?"

"No, man, it's cool," he said. "Just control your date."

I half expected Lucas to correct him, but he didn't say anything. I knew he and his buddies had come to the dance without dates. And he knew I was with Matt. But he kept moving really close to me during the next song, and a few times I bumped up against him. It was so crowded in the room that I couldn't help it. At least that was what I told myself.

But I knew that after the first few times, I brushed up against him on purpose. I knew he was turned on, and so was I. And I knew I should have stayed away from him, but I didn't. I checked to see if Matt was watching me from the next room, but he was still talking to the same guy.

At one point I lit a cigarette and danced with it, twirling around carelessly. A few people moved away and told me to be careful or I'd burn someone.

I just laughed. So did Lucas.

When we were leaning against a wall, taking a breather, Tricia came over to me and said, "Karen, where are you putting your ashes? You better not burn my parents' floor."

I just shrugged and laughed.

"I'm serious. There are ashtrays around. Use one, okay?" she said before someone grabbed her arm and pulled her away.

"Yeah, Karen, use an ashtray," Lucas mimicked.

"Okay," I said. And I turned around and grabbed the first thing I saw, which was a glass dish filled with red and green M&M's. It was heavier than it looked—I guess it was crystal or something. I lifted it over my head and dumped the candy all over the floor and shouted, "It's snowing!"

Lucas thought it was so hilarious he practically collapsed on the floor. "C'mon," he said. "I need another drink. Want one?"

I followed him to the kitchen, still carrying the candy dish. On the way, I spied a sprig of mistletoe in the doorway. I nudged Lucas. "Hey," I said, pointing upward. "Look."

"Uh-oh. I better kiss you," he said and leaned toward me.

His breath was hot, and he tasted like whiskey. He grabbed my arm. "Come on," he said and pulled me toward the kitchen.

That was when the candy dish slipped out of my hands, fell to the floor, and broke.

"Oops," I said and shrugged. Lucas started laughing. I kicked a piece of glass so that it skittered across the polished wood.

"God, Karen, what are you doing?" I heard Gina ask, somewhere nearby.

I giggled and looked at Lucas.

"Come on, let's go get a drink," he said, and I let him pull me away.

"Where are we going?" I asked.

"Down to the basement. That's where Tricia's dad keeps all the good stuff. Come on."

He led me through the kitchen to a door in the back entryway. I looked over my shoulder and didn't see Matt anywhere. Lucas turned on a light, and I followed him down into a finished basement. There was a pool table and a stereo and a couch.

"Have a seat," Lucas said, motioning toward the couch.

"But I—oh, well, why not." I plunked down. I mean, it wasn't like there was anything else to do. Matt had been ignoring me. He hadn't even come looking for me.

Lucas opened a cupboard in one corner and started rummaging through some bottles. "A hundred and fifty proof," he announced, holding one up. He grabbed two shot glasses and carried everything over to the couch. He set the stuff down, then reached back and turned on the radio.

I watched while Lucas poured some of the amber liquid into a shot glass.

"Drink up," he said, handing me the shot glass.

"No, thanks," I said, feeling way too wild already. "You have mine."

"Sure?"

"No, thanks."

Lucas downed the drink in one gulp, then poured himself two more shots. I stood up.

"Hey, where are you going?" Lucas asked.

"No place," I said.

I bounced my leg to the beat of the music, then grabbed Lucas's hand and said, "Let's dance!"

I don't remember when Lucas shut off the lights. Or when he pulled me down on the couch and we started kissing. But suddenly the lights went on again. I blinked and jerked away from Lucas. What was I doing?

Matt stood at the foot of the stairs, staring at Lucas and me, our coats in his hand. He hurled my coat to the floor, turned around, and slammed the door behind him.

"Matt!" I grabbed my coat and dashed after him up the stairs. "Matt, wait! Please," I wailed. "Please let me explain."

He whirled around, his face distorted in fury. "What's to explain? I come with my girl to a party. She goes downstairs and makes out with another guy. You make me sick!"

"But Matt! I wasn't . . ."

"Shut up! You'll wake up the whole neighborhood!"

"Please don't be so mean," I wailed. "Please let me explain!"

He turned around to look at me. "Okay," he said. "Explain."

I just stood there and talked. I had no idea what I was saying. I said I was sorry. And that I really liked him and wanted to talk to him all night, but it was just so hard. It came out like gibberish, but I couldn't seem to control my mouth with my brain.

He cut me off. "You really are crazy, Karen, aren't you?" Then he turned his back on me and walked away, shaking his head.

"I am not crazy!" I screeched after him.

I walked home in a cold, stinging rain by myself.

6

Sunday, December 12

The first thing I did when I woke up Sunday morning was cringe.

Oh, God. What had I done last night?

I forced myself to replay the entire scene at the party—at least as much as I remembered.

A lot of what had happened after I had dropped that candy dish was a blur. I lay in bed, trying to piece things together.

No matter how fuzzy the rest of the party was, the words Matt had flung at me when he'd stormed away echoed loud and clear in my mind.

"You really are crazy, Karen, aren't you?"

Those words still stung.

I remembered how furious I'd been when he said it. And even now when I realized that some of what I'd done *had* been a little crazy, I was angry.

I am not crazy, I told myself, sitting up in bed and frowning.

Not like my mother.

I turned toward my bedside table and saw the envelope I'd tossed there last night. It had been propped up against my pillow when I got home, and my name was written on the front in my mother's almost illegible scrawl. I hadn't bothered with it then. I'd been too upset.

Now, though, I reached for it and slid my finger under the flap.

I pulled out a piece of paper on which she'd scrawled a few lines, and something else fluttered out onto the floor. It was money—a hundred-dollar bill.

I picked it up and read my mother's note.

Dear Karen—

I just want to say I'm sorry about the job interview. Here's something for your shopping trip into Boston with Gina tomorrow. Splurge on something for yourself.

Love,
Mom

P.S. This is just between us, okay?

I scowled. Translated, the postscript meant, *"Don't tell Daddy."*

For a moment I debated not taking the money—tossing it and her stupid note into the garbage.

Then I came to my senses. Why shouldn't I take the money? It didn't mean I'd forgiven my mother. She couldn't buy me.

While we were waiting for the train to Boston, I asked Gina if she was upset with me.

"Why would I be upset? I'm not the one who broke a candy dish and had a screaming fight with her date." She smiled to soften the effect of her words. "How did you get home?"

"Don't worry, I got home. And I really don't feel like talking about it."

Gina acted a little hurt, and I felt bad, but I really didn't want to talk about it. It was no big deal, anyway. Matt and I weren't right for each other. *It's his loss,* I told myself during the hour ride into Boston's South Station.

Every so often I glanced out the window. The temperature was in the twenties and the sun was dazzling on the ice that coated every tree and wire and bush.

As we started to get into the city, the train slowed down. We were creeping through those gritty industrial areas on the outskirts when I started to feel uneasy. I couldn't concentrate and kept looking around anxiously, convinced something was going to happen.

Something bad.

That I was going to die.

And the more I worried, the slower the train went. I felt as though the car were closing in on me, but there was no place for me to go, and besides, what would people think?

Gina just sat there oblivious, licking her index finger each time she turned a page of her *Sassy*.

The train went into a tunnel, then it slowed and stopped with grinding and screeching sounds.

I poked Gina.

"What?" she asked, glancing up from the magazine.

"Why do you think we've stopped?"

She looked out the window, as though she hadn't even realized it. Then she frowned and shrugged, as if to say, *No big deal.*

I just looked at her, swallowing hard, waiting.

"I don't know—red signal?" she finally offered. "Why? What's wrong? Do you have to go to the bathroom or something?"

"Yeah," I muttered and turned back toward the window. There was nothing to see. We were stuck in the tunnel, and I was approaching all-out panic.

I'd never been claustrophobic. But I felt as though I couldn't breathe. I was suffocating. I kept twisting my hands around in my lap, and they were all clammy. My entire body was tense.

Something was going to happen.

I started picturing the tunnel collapsing, burying the train. Was that why we were stopped? Because they had found out the tunnel was unstable, and they were afraid to keep moving? *Oh, God.* What if the tunnel was under the river right now? I pictured the car we were in being crushed under massive beams, and then water pouring in, drowning us.

Suddenly the train lurched and started moving again. It built up speed. I took huge gulps of air and let them out slowly, trying to calm myself.

Within minutes we were out of the tunnel and pulling into the station. I felt better.

Gina sighed, dropped her magazine into her shoulder bag, and looked at me. "All set?"

"Yup."

"You want to make a pit stop in the station before we head for the stores, right?"

"Um, right." I couldn't believe she hadn't noticed what I had just gone through.

What *had* I just gone through? The anxiety had disappeared as abruptly as it had come. Nothing like that had ever happened to me before.

Gina slung her bag over her shoulder and zipped her jacket. "Come on, let's go."

She headed off the train, and I followed, still feeling a little wobbly.

Filene's Basement was jammed. Gina and I decided to split up so we'd get more shopping done. We picked a record store we both knew was nearby and agreed to meet in two hours.

I went upstairs to the main department store, which was still crowded but more civilized than the bargain basement. As I walked through the women's clothing department, I spotted a great blouse I just knew Gina would love. The collar and cuffs were edged in expensive lace, not that cheap synthetic kind that looks so tacky. And there were tiny pink rosebuds hand-embroidered on the curved collar. I looked at the price tag: $129.99. I bought it without thinking twice.

As I handed my money over to the saleswoman, I felt a little twinge of regret. It was a lot of money for a blouse. And Gina and I had set a twenty-dollar limit on our Christmas presents for each other. I had been planning to get her a sheer floral scarf and a paperback.

But Gina would *love* this blouse. I thought about how good it would make her feel to wear something so beautiful. She always complained about her wardrobe —Mrs. Petrillo sewed a lot of her clothes to save money.

I found myself browsing through cashmere sweaters that were outrageously expensive even at twenty-five percent off.

I was dying to buy one for myself. It would be an investment, after all. A person could wear a good cashmere sweater for years.

I held up a soft black sweater and looked in a mirror.

"That's on sale today. And it looks great with your coloring," a voice said, and I turned to see a pretty salesperson standing behind me.

"It does?"

"Yes. And with your figure, it'll look terrific. Want to try it on?"

"No, thanks." I didn't feel patient enough to go into the dressing room and take off my heavy coat and all the layers of clothing I was wearing.

"Well, you look like a perfect size seven, anyway," the salesgirl said.

"Exactly," I said, running my fingers over the luxurious fabric.

She stood watching me. "You have a string of good pearls, right?"

"Right," I lied.

"Well, all you need is this sweater and pearls, and you've got a classic outfit that goes anywhere."

"Right," I said again.

I pictured myself in the sweater and pearls—I'd get some of those eventually—sitting at a desk in a New York City classroom, designing fashions.

"Will you hold this for me?" I asked the girl abruptly. "I'll be back for it in a little while."

She smiled. "Sure."

Ten minutes later I was standing in line at an ATM machine in a bank lobby down the street. Clutched in my hand was the plastic bank card for the savings account I'd had since I was a baby. When I went away on a weekend trip with the Petrillos last summer, my father had given it to me. "In case of an emergency," he'd said. I hadn't needed it, and he'd never asked for it back.

I knew there was about four thousand dollars in the account, all my birthday and Christmas money from my grandparents, and First Communion money, any cash I had received over the years. I knew it was for college.

But I needed it *now*.

And it wasn't as if I wouldn't replace the money.

I'd start putting it back as soon as I got my job, which would be any day now.

In less than a minute I was holding five hundred dollars in cash.

Back on the street, I was unable to stop smiling as I hurried toward Filene's and my cashmere sweater.

"Hey! You look different. What'd you do?"

"I had a makeover at one of the cosmetic counters in Jordan Marsh. Do you like it?"

I'd found Gina in the record store looking at the R.E.M. CDs. She looked closely at my face. "The eye makeup's a little heavy for daytime, don't you think?"

"I told them to make it dramatic. I bought everything they used on me, see?" I asked, holding up a bag.

"Wasn't it expensive?"

I shrugged. "My mother gave me some extra money so that I could treat myself to something, so I did. I got a gorgeous sweater, too."

"Really?" Gina asked, and glanced down at the bags I was holding. She poked the biggest one. "What did you buy in a sporting goods store?"

"Your present."

She looked up at me and saw that I was teasing. She always said she was the least athletic person on the face of the earth.

"Actually," I told her, "it's a tennis racket for my father. A good one."

"I didn't know he plays tennis."

"He doesn't. But he plays racquetball, so I figured he'd probably like tennis, too, if he tried it."

Gina frowned. "But don't you think—"

"And look at what I got for my mother in one of the jewelry stores down the block," I said, setting down my bags at my feet and digging through one until I found the small paper bag from the jeweler's. I opened it, pulled out the small velvet box, and snapped it open.

Gina leaned in to see the pair of pearl earrings inside. "Wow—are those real?"

"Of course they're real."

"How could you afford them?"

"The guy gave me a deal," I said briefly. "I have your present, too. But I still haven't found anything for Ethan. I saw a basketball hoop in the sporting goods store, and I know he needs one, but—"

"Karen," Gina interrupted. "A *basketball* hoop? How are you going to carry something that gigantic?"

I shrugged. "You'd help me?"

"Karen . . ."

"Please, Gina? Please?"

She sighed. "Well, can we eat lunch before you get it? It's almost three o'clock, and I'm starving."

"Okay. Let's go to this Japanese restaurant I just saw a few blocks from here. I'm dying for sushi."

"Oh, ick." Gina made a face.

"C'mon, Gina."

"But I can't eat raw fish."

"So? That's not the only thing they have there. You can get tempura or something. My treat," I added.

She sighed. "All right. I'm too hungry to stand here arguing. Let's go."

My father picked us up at the station. After we had dropped Gina off and pulled into our driveway, I saw a Christmas tree leaning against the garage.

"Hey," I said. "Where did that come from?"

My father frowned. "I don't know."

We've always had an artificial tree, although I begged year after year for a real one. The Petrillos always get a real tree, and I love the way their whole house smells—all Christmasy and cozy.

My mother always said real trees made too much mess with the sap and dropped needles. Either she'd changed her mind, or Santa had delivered the tree.

I collected my bags from the trunk and my father stashed the basketball hoop in the garage in case Ethan was around. Neither of us mentioned the tree as we trudged past it. I followed my father through the snow, up the steps, across the deck, to the door.

My mother was in the kitchen, and when I saw what she was doing, I nearly fell over.

Baking.

She was baking cookies.

My mother hadn't made Christmas cookies since Ethan and I were little. She said it was too much work.

But now it looked as if she was in a baking frenzy. The table and counters were lined with strips of waxed paper upon which sat gingerbread boys and cherry bonbons and sugar cookies in the shapes of snowmen and candy canes and fat Santas. There were mixing bowls and cookie sheets everywhere, and the kitchen smelled wonderful—like butter and vanilla and spices.

She had carols blasting on the stereo, and she'd apparently lugged the boxes marked "X-mas Decorations" down from the attic. I could see them stacked in the other room.

My father was as astonished as I was.

"What are you *doing,* Sheila?" he asked.

"Making merry," she said gaily, and she actually went over and gave him a big kiss.

She turned to me. "Did you see the tree, Karen?"

I just nodded, still too surprised to say anything.

"I was out shopping, and I got into such a festive mood that I thought, Why not? I stopped at the hardware store and bought one of those stands for it, too." She kept jabbering on in a rush, telling us every detail.

My father was speechless.

"But I thought you said real trees made too much mess," I said finally.

"So? We'll clean it up."

We just gaped at her.

Then my father walked toward her.

I flinched, wondering what he was going to do. I couldn't take it if they had another screaming argument right now and ruined everything.

Breathlessly, I watched as he leaned toward my mother—and cupped her chin in his hand.

"C'mere," he said in a gentle tone I rarely heard him use with her anymore.

"What?" she asked, and I noticed that her eyes were all sparkly.

"You've got some frosting on your cheek."

He rubbed it off with his finger.

And I just stood there watching them, suddenly happy enough to burst.

7

Monday, December 13

Matt was in homeroom. I saw him sitting there, talking to Darren Westing as soon as I walked in. He tried to ignore me, but I caught him looking at me a few times. He didn't seem exactly thrilled to see me, but he didn't seem mad, either. More like—sad. And puzzled.

And I don't know what happened to my vow not to let him bother me, but all of a sudden I felt awful. About everything.

As soon as the bell rang, I jumped up and ran out into the hall to get away from him.

All I could think was that I had to avoid him. I

wasn't going to let him ruin my day. I was still flying high from last night.

We had spent it as a family, decorating the tree. I even coaxed Ethan out of his room to help, and after a while he relaxed, and we had a great time. And if my mother went a little crazy with the decorations, heaping tinsel everywhere and insisting on adding extra strings of lights, well, it was no big deal.

After we'd lit the tree and marveled at how beautiful it was, my parents went to the family room together to watch a movie. Usually—on the rare nights when he was home—my father watched TV in their bedroom and my mother stayed in the family room. But last night it was like they were on a date or something.

I spent some time in Ethan's room, listening to his new Smashing Pumpkins CD. Then when he got tired and I was still too keyed up to sleep, I'd gone into my room to wrap presents. After they were all wrapped, I'd stayed up until four in the morning, rereading *A Christmas Carol* until I finally drifted off.

The next day I walked into the cafeteria at lunchtime to find Gina waiting at our usual table. "I have something to tell you, and I don't want you to be mad at me for not saying anything earlier."

"What is it?"

"Um, Saturday morning, when I went to my grandmother's?" She seemed hesitant.

"Yeah?" I said impatiently. *"What?"*

"My uncle Mario was there. You know—my mother's older brother—the one who owns the Italian restaurant?"

"Right, I know who he is. What about him?"

"He just added on another room, and business is booming. So he needs to hire more help. . . ."

"And?—Oh!" I exclaimed, suddenly getting it. "He could hire *us!*"

"He *could* . . ."

"But he won't?"

"No, it's not that, Karen. I'm just not sure it'd work out."

"Why not?" I asked, my mind racing. I would be the best waitress that restaurant had ever seen so that I could make lots of tips and save hundreds of dollars to go to Italy.

"You know," Gina said.

I noticed she was acting uncomfortable. "No, actually I don't."

"I just—I know how you are sometimes, Karen. You get kind of . . . distracted."

I frowned. "Distracted?"

"I mean, you get all excited about something, and then suddenly you lose interest. You really want a job *now,* but what if you change your mind?"

"I won't," I insisted. "This would work out really well, Gina. For both of us. It would be perfect!"

"My uncle will only hire us if he feels he can count on us. We can't let him down."

"We won't."

"Well then, after school we can meet him at the restaurant."

"Today?"

"Yup. Why? Can't you make it?"

"Sure I can," I assured her, deciding I'd have to blow off the magazine staff meeting. In fact, I hadn't even finished sorting through the stuff I was supposed to have edited this afternoon.

But what was more important? Some stupid extra-curricular project, or a real job?

"This is going to be great." I smiled at Gina, reached past my mostly untouched lasagna, and lifted my skimmed-milk carton in a toast. "Here's to our new jobs. Italy, here we come!"

"Italy, here *you* come. I still haven't said I would go," Gina said. But she lifted her carton, too, and hit it against mine.

After school we walked the few blocks to Mario's. Gina's uncle was a short, jolly man who kept pinching our cheeks. He talked to us for like, five minutes, telling us what we could expect. Hard work, long hours, and—the only part I really paid attention to—decent tips.

"Well?" he asked, folding his arms on the red- and white-checked cloth and gazing expectantly at us across the table.

Gina and I looked at each other, then back at him.

"Sounds great!" I said enthusiastically.

"Gina Marie?" he asked, turning to her.

"Great," she echoed.

"All right, then."

"We're hired?" I asked.

"Have you checked with your parents to see if it's all right?"

"Are you kidding? They'd love it if I had my own source of income. Then I'll stop bugging them for money."

"In that case, you're hired," he said.

I squealed. "You mean, like today?" I asked excitedly. I couldn't wait to start bringing in money.

Mario laughed and pinched my cheek. "That's what I like to see. A girl who isn't afraid to roll up her sleeves and work."

I shot a triumphant glance at Gina that said, *See?*

"No," her uncle went on, "not today. Monday is Ziti Fest. It's too crazy in here for me to have time to train you. But tomorrow." He nodded. "Be here after school, same time as today."

Out on the sidewalk, which was slushy from the melting snow, I gave Gina an enormous hug. "Thank you, thank you, thank you!" I said. "I'm so psyched about this job. I can't wait to start!"

"Yeah, me, too," she said.

I couldn't help noticing that she still was acting a little dubious, though. "Don't worry, Gina," I said to reassure her. "I'm going to be the best, most dedicated, hardworking waitress your uncle ever hired!"

8

Tuesday, December 14

Halfway through the pop quiz in social studies, I put down my pen abruptly and stood up. Everyone looked at me.

"Yes? Is something wrong, Karen?" asked Mr. Dexter, the teacher. He was a small, nervous type.

"Can I please have a hall pass?" I asked.

"A hall pass? For what?"

"The ladies' room," I said. It was the first thing that came to me. "I have to go. Bad," I added for good measure.

What was he supposed to say to that? Of course he gave me the pass. I snatched it out of his fingers on my way to the door.

Mr. Dexter looked doubtfully at my bookbag, which I had brought with me. I thought he was going to ask me about it, but he didn't. I guess maybe he thought I had some Tampax or aspirin or something in there, something I would need in the bathroom. All he said was, "Hurry back, Karen, or you won't have enough time to finish your quiz."

"I will." Yeah, right. I couldn't stand sitting there another minute. Who cared about some stupid quiz?

I walked briskly down the hall, practically running. I needed to burn off some energy. Actually, it was funny that I had so much energy, considering that I had gotten only three hours of sleep last night.

Now, in school, I felt just as restless as I had when I was tossing and turning in bed. I didn't want to sit in some stupid chair and listen to some stupid teacher talk about some stupid subject. I wanted to—I don't know what I wanted to do.

Just—*something*.

So I did. I cut the rest of social studies—spent it wandering the halls, waving my pass at any hall monitor who gave me a suspicious look. And then, the entire forty-two minutes when I should have been sharing a lab table with Matt, I was hanging in the grungy girls' bathroom in the A building, bumming cigarettes from the handful of regulars. I didn't think twice about it, didn't worry about getting nabbed.

When the bell rang, I bummed an extra butt and matches from Patty Lawrence and tucked them into my bookbag. Then I went off to the cafeteria to meet Gina.

Seventh period I went to art, which I would never, ever skip. I tried to sketch a still life, but I kept messing up. Every time I ripped a page out of my sketchpad, crumpled it up, and threw it into the wastebasket, everybody stared at me like there was something wrong.

"Bad art day," I finally explained to the silent room, and cracked myself up. Nobody else seemed to think it was funny, and Mrs. Rosenbaum acted concerned.

The door opened and an office messenger walked in and handed a folded note to Mrs. Rosenbaum. I thought he shot a smug glance in my direction on his way out. Or was it my imagination?

Mrs. Rosenbaum read the note, looked up, and said, "Karen?"

I guess the little twerp *had* been looking at me.

"Yeah?" I asked, my charcoal pencil still poised on the paper.

"Mr. O'Neill would like to see you."

There was a low, taunting "ooooh" from a couple of the boys in the back of the room. O'Neill was the vice principal, who happened to be in charge of detention. Everyone knew what a summons to his office meant.

Unfazed, I stood up and started for the door.

"Better take your books and things," Mrs. Rosenbaum said quietly. I wasn't the type who got called out of class. Not like Patty Lawrence and her friends, who, when they weren't in the bathroom, were usually waiting on the bench outside of O'Neill's office.

I went back for my stuff, then headed for the door again, flashing Mrs. Rosenbaum a smile to show her that it was no big deal. She didn't smile back.

O'Neill, a balding, beady-eyed little man, was waiting at his desk. "Have a seat, Miss Spencer. Do you know why you're here?"

Obviously my biology teacher had sent a cut slip on me. But I just shrugged and said, "No."

"Is there a valid reason you weren't in biology this morning?"

I just looked at him.

"Well?"

I shrugged.

He sighed. "Karen, this is not the kind of behavior I expect from someone like you. I know that you're not—" Just then his phone rang. He picked it up. "Yes? . . . Yes, but can it wait a few minutes? . . . All right. . . . I'll be right in."

He hung up, stood up, and said, "Excuse me a moment, please." He closed the door behind him.

I waited, thrumming my fingertips on the chair arm and looking around. It was a boring office—no family pictures, even though everyone knew he was married and had kids. No plants or anything.

I wished I could smoke the cigarette in my purse. Even a puff or two would help. I spotted an ashtray on O'Neill's desk. It was filled with paperclips. Still . . .

Before I could think twice, I had dumped the contents onto the desk and taken the butt and a pack of matches out of my bag. I put the cigarette between my lips and hesitated for only the briefest moment before lighting up.

I told myself I'd take two puffs, then put it out. O'Neill would never know. I had smoked half the cigarette before the door burst open and O'Neill was standing there.

"I *thought* I smelled *smoke!* What are you *doing,* Karen?"

Somewhere deep inside me, a little voice warned that I was in real trouble now. I ignored it.

He snatched the cigarette out of my hand, stubbed it out in the ashtray, then slammed the door. "Not only," he said, his voice shaking slightly, "do you have the usual one-day detention for cutting a class. You have three weeks of detention for smoking that cigarette. Starting this afternoon."

Still feeling pretty detached, I was about to shrug. But instead, somehow, I burst into tears.

O'Neill was so surprised that for a moment he just stared. Then he cleared his throat and said, "All right, uh, calm down."

"I . . . can't," I sobbed. I started talking a mile a minute even through my tears, telling him how important my new job was, and I think I even started in about Italy.

He kept handing me tissues and waiting for me to calm down.

I don't know where that torrent of tears and words came from, but once I got started, it wasn't easy to stop. Finally my sobs died down and I managed to finish, "So I just can't have detention today."

He was frowning. "You should have thought of that before you cut class. And what on earth possessed you to light a cigarette in my office, Karen?"

"I don't know," I wailed, burying my face in my hands.

When I looked up, I couldn't believe what I saw. Mr. O'Neill had softened. He was looking at me with sympathetic eyes. "All right, stop crying now," he said in a quiet voice.

I sniffled miserably and tried to catch my breath.

"Karen," he said when I'd quieted down, "I'm very concerned. Not only did you cut class, but I pulled your file and your grades are slipping badly. Is something wrong? Something at home?"

"No!" I protested so loudly that he winced.

He just stared at me for a long time before saying, "I'm going to make a deal with you. I'll let you off the hook this time—"

"Oh, thank you!"

"On one condition."

I blew my nose again. "What is it?"

"You have to talk to Miss Rand. I'll set up an appointment."

Miss Rand was the school psychologist. What did he think? I was nuts?

"I don't need to see her," I informed him coldly.

He shrugged. "Well, that's the deal. Either you go with the three weeks of detention, starting today, or you see Miss Rand."

I thought about it. There was no way I could not show up at Mario's this afternoon, not after what Gina had said about me. I had to prove I was reliable.

But—a psychologist?

Again, a little warning bell went off in the back of my mind, and I thought about my mother. And the other person whose image kept poking at my mind lately—my aunt Jill.

But I wouldn't let *her* in. She had nothing to do with me.

"Well?" O'Neill asked, steepling his fingers and watching me.

Miss Rand was young and pretty and sweet. In fact, she was related to the Murdocks, whose kids I used to baby-sit before they moved away. I certainly wasn't about to tell her anything. But then, there was no law that said I had to, was there? I could go see her and not say a word.

I looked at Mr. O'Neill.

"You win," I said sullenly. "I'll go see Miss Rand."

9

Wednesday, December 15

I was almost late for biology. When I got there everyone was sitting down, and I caught Matt expectantly watching the door, as if he was waiting for me.

He turned away quickly and pretended to be reading his book when I sat down.

Mrs. Nisely was just beginning to pass out papers when the door opened and an office messenger walked in. She gave Mrs. Nisely a folded slip of paper.

The teacher looked at it, then said, "Karen?"

"Yes?"

She held the note up expectantly. "This is for you."

Frowning, I got up and darted forward to get it.

When I sat down and Mrs. Nisely started talking again, I read it. I could tell that Matt was trying to sneak a peek at it, so I tilted it away.

All it said was "Please report to Miss Rand's office after lunch period," and it was signed by Mr. O'Neill.

My hands started trembling as soon as I read it. I went to tuck it into my purse, which was hanging on the back of my chair, but it slipped out of my fingers and fluttered to the floor.

Matt started to bend over like he was going to pick it up, but I leaned over and grabbed it.

It had landed faceup, and I knew he must have seen what it said.

Oh, well, I thought as I shoved it into the pocket of my jeans instead. *Who cares what he thinks?*

He'd already accused me of being nuts.

Now he'd just think I really was.

When the bell rang, I immediately jumped up and started for the door when I felt someone's fingers on my sleeve.

I spun around and saw Matt. "What?" I asked, agitated.

"I just . . ." He looked uncomfortable.

"What?"

"Nothing," he said and let go of me.

I scooted away, not looking back.

I debated not going to the cafeteria, but I had a pounding headache and knew Gina would have aspirin in her purse.

She was waiting for me at our usual table, and as

soon as I got there, I said, "Listen, Gina, do you have any aspirin? My head is killing me."

"Sure." She reached into her purse and took out a little white plastic bottle.

I opened it, spilled some tablets into my palm, and tried to raise them to my mouth.

Gina grabbed my hand. "Karen!"

"What?"

"You can't take *four* of those."

"Gina, my head is splitting."

She grabbed two back and said, "Come on, let's get in line. You can't swallow them without drinking anything."

"Yes, I can," I said, and I did.

She just shook her head but didn't say anything.

We both got the hot lunch, sloppy joes, but I barely touched mine. I wasn't hungry. My mind was on the appointment with Miss Rand.

Twice Gina interrupted her chatter about how much she hated gym class to ask me if I was *sure* I was all right.

Both times I fought the urge to snap at her and only said, "I'm fine, except for this headache."

When we were on our way out of the cafeteria, heading for geometry, which was the one class we shared, I realized I'd have to tell her what was going on.

"Uh, Gina," I said as people talked and walked and slammed locker doors all around us. "I'm not going to geometry."

"How come? Karen, you better not be cutting again." She knew about Tuesday. Word gets around fast.

"I'm not. I just have to be someplace else, that's all."

"Where?"

"I have to see Miss Rand," I mumbled.

"What?" She leaned closer. "I can't hear you."

"I said"—I took a deep breath—"I have to see Miss Rand."

Her eyes widened. "Why?"

I shrugged. "Mr. O'Neill is making me."

"Are you okay, Karen?" she asked, studying me. "'Cause if you're not, you can tell me. I mean, you've been acting sort of different—"

"Don't worry about me," I said, brushing her off.

She studied me closely again. Then all she said was, "Do you want me to let McCann know why you're not in geometry?"

"No. The office takes care of that, I guess. Listen, I'll see you later, okay?"

"Okay."

I hurried down the hall and bumped smack into Howard Pepper, the editor of the literary magazine.

"Karen," he said, "I tried to track you down yesterday. Didn't Matt tell you I was looking for you?"

"Uh, no," I said. "But I can't talk now."

He shoved his glasses up on his nose and narrowed his watery blue eyes at me. "Well, all I need to know is where that stuff for the January issue is. You were supposed to hand it in at Monday's meeting, which you conveniently missed."

"I had a job interview."

"So? You could have dropped your stuff off. Unless, of course, you don't have it ready."

I decided I hated Howard. "It's ready."

"Well, can you hand it over?"

"I don't have it with me."

"Well, let's get it out of your locker then."

"It's at home. I forgot it."

"Karen, what am I supposed to do now? I've got to have that stuff at the typesetter's by Monday afternoon. And I need to look it over first."

"So? I'll give it to you Monday morning."

"That's not good enough."

"Oh, really? Well, guess what, Howard? That's your problem, not mine. Because as of now, I quit. See ya."

I brushed by him and ran off down the hall.

In fact, I ran right past Rand's office. I just couldn't deal with her right now.

I'll worry about it on Monday, I told myself.

10

Friday, December 17

Mario had decided that for the first few weeks, Gina and I would work every other day, until we were both fully trained. Today was Gina's day, so I walked home alone.

I started thinking about Matt as I walked briskly through the chilly December air. About how he'd tried to talk to me after biology. And how he had seen that note telling me to see the psychologist.

I knew he thought I was crazy. Crazy. Like my aunt Jill. Is that what he thought? He didn't know me at all. Who did he think he was, anyway?

But still, I kept thinking about the expression in his

eyes when he'd stopped me after class. He'd looked—I don't know, sympathetic? Not that I wanted sympathy, from him or anyone else. But still . . .

A photograph in the plate-glass window of the beauty salon I was passing caught my eye. I stopped to examine it. The model had a pixie-ish look, with small features and short, swingy hair. It was a blunt cut tucked behind her ears, with a fringe of bangs around the forehead.

For a moment I just stood there on the street, studying the picture. Then I opened the door and hurried into the salon.

"Karen? Is that you?" I heard my mother call from her bedroom as I clomped down the upstairs hall, shrugging out of my jacket.

"Yeah," was all I said.

My mother stuck her head out into the hallway. "Mike just called."

"Oh."

"He said to call—" Then she broke off and gasped. "Karen! What did you do to your—"

"I got it cut," I snapped.

"I can see that."

"Go ahead, Mom, tell me it looks lousy."

"But it doesn't. Actually, it looks adorable. I was just surprised. I didn't know you were going to get a haircut."

Neither did I, I thought grimly, opening the door of my room and flinging my coat on the floor.

What had gotten into me?

One second I'd been standing on the street, and the next I was in a swivel chair telling some girl with teased hair to chop off all my hair.

I didn't realize it was a mistake until it was too late and piles of wavy light brown strands were lying at my feet.

The girl in the mirror looked like a stranger.

"I love it!" the beautician squealed.

I hate it was my immediate reaction.

I looked like a boy.

"It makes those pretty hazel eyes of yours look huge," she kept saying as she fluffed it up under the blow dryer.

Now my mother said the exact same thing. "It really makes your eyes stand out, Karen," she said from the doorway of my room.

"It does not."

"Yes, it does. What's the matter?"

I opened my mouth to snap *Nothing!* but burst into tears instead.

My mother wrapped her arms around me. "Don't cry, honey."

"But I look so ugly."

"You do not. You look beautiful."

"No, I don't. I look like a Q-Tip."

My mother sounded like she was trying not to laugh

when she said, "Oh, Karen, you don't look like a Q-Tip."

"Yes, I do. Look at it . . . it's all puffy. What did she do to me? I wanted a blunt cut—not this bouffant."

Now my mother laughed.

"It's not funny," I sobbed.

"Oh, Karen, don't worry. All you need to do is restyle it, use some gel or something to smooth it out. It'll look great."

I sniffled. "You think so?"

"Sure." She patted my shoulder. "Come on, I'll help you."

And she did.

My hair did look better after she finished with it. It was sleek and tucked behind my ears in a pixie style, more like I had imagined.

Later, my mother and I ate takeout Chinese food in front of "Wheel of Fortune." Then I went upstairs and took out a bunch of poems I'd written a few months ago, when I was depressed.

I sat there and looked at the first poem. It was called "Are You My Mother?"

> You torture me with jagged words like teeth
> hacking at my tender soul
> then leaving it to rot

I must have read those lines over about a dozen times without really seeing them. My mind kept wandering.

I thought about Matt. And my haircut. And how nice and normal my mother had been.

I didn't even realize, until I had put the untouched poems away and was lying in bed trying to fall asleep after midnight, that she wasn't supposed to be home in the afternoon.

She should have been at work.

Monday, December 20

Waitressing wasn't exactly as easy as I'd thought it would be. I mean, those trays are way heavier than they look, and you have to balance them on your shoulder and try not to spill. Gina had a tougher time getting the hang of it than I did, probably because she's weaker.

By last night, after my second day of working, I was physically exhausted. My lack of sleep was finally catching up with me. But I was on a high, exhilarated about the more than hundred dollars in tips I'd gotten since I started working.

Mario had told me that a customer said I had

provided the fastest service he'd ever had. I was glowing, and so was Mario.

That praise, and the money, almost made my memories of the horrendous Friday I'd had at school fade away. I'd almost forgotten about Matt. And cutting classes. And Miss Rand. But everything started coming back to me Monday morning. And I just couldn't handle it.

Which was why, after homeroom, I headed straight to the girls' bathroom. I let the door swing shut behind me and carelessly dumped my books on the edge of the sink. They fell in and I let them, not caring that the steady drip of water from the faucet was going to soak them. I reached into my purse and pulled out a pack of cigarettes. I lit up and was glad I had the bathroom to myself. I hung out in there all through first period and second. Whenever someone came in, I'd hide my cigarette, make sure it wasn't a teacher, and then puff away again.

I was still sitting there, smoking and reading the *Enquirer*, when the door opened again and the girls' gym teacher walked in. She took one look at me, narrowed her eyes, and I knew I was in trouble.

I had been sitting on the bench outside O'Neill's office for an hour when my mother showed up.

"Hi, Mom," I said cheerfully.

Mrs. Rivera looked up and said, "Mrs. Spencer?"

"That's right," she said, not thrilled with me or with being here. "You called at my office and said Mr.

O'Neill needed to see me right away. I hope this is urgent because my boss wasn't happy with me leaving, and I really need my job."

Oh, she's setting it up to blame me when she gets fired this time, I thought, shaking my head. As if she hadn't already missed all those days.

Mrs. Rivera ushered my mother and me into O'Neill's office.

"Mrs. Spencer, I'm so glad you could come down. Won't you please have a seat? You, too, Karen," he said.

My mother got right to the point. "What seems to be the problem?"

"I'm concerned, Mrs. Spencer, about the change in Karen. She was one of our brightest students. Recently, however, her grades have gone from *A*s and *B*s to *D*s and an *F*—"

"Who gave me an *F?*" I cut in. "It wasn't Mrs. Nisely, was it? Because if it was—"

"Karen!" Mr. O'Neill said, swiveling back toward my mother. "This is exactly what I'm talking about, Mrs. Spencer. Karen has been displaying disruptive, inappropriate behavior in some of her classes. She has been cutting class and smoking in the girls' lavatory. And she broke her appointment with our school psychologist on Friday, without giving—"

Now it was my mother's turn to interrupt. "School psychiatrist? Why are you sending my daughter to a shrink?"

He seemed a bit startled by her tone. "Mrs. Spencer, it's routine when this type of thing happens. I assure you that Miss Rand is qualified to—"

"I'm sure she is, too—to take care of kids who have *real* problems. My daughter doesn't need a psychologist. Karen has been very stressed out lately, what with her new job, and school, and boy troubles."

I winced at that.

My mother reached over and patted my arm, still looking at O'Neill. "I promise you, Mr. O'Neill, that I will handle this. Karen and I will have a long talk as soon as we get home. You'll see a change in her tomorrow. I guarantee it."

He hesitated, then shrugged. "All right, Mrs. Spencer. I'll leave this in your hands. Take her home now. But if Karen—"

"She won't," my mother said, staring at me. "Will you, Karen?"

"No," I said. "I won't." Whatever *that* meant.

The first thing my mother asked when we got to the car was, "Do you mind if we stop at Peaberry's for a cup of coffee before we go home?"

"Huh?" I saw that she was smiling at me across the front seat.

What was going on? Only two minutes ago she'd been angry at me. Now she'd done a Jekyll and Hyde and was saying conspiratorially, "I really want a cup of hazelnut coffee."

"I thought you were taking me home to deal with me."

"I just said it so ol' Baldy would get off our backs."

"Baldy?" I cracked up at that.

She laughed, too, as she backed the car out and quickly maneuvered through the school parking lot and out onto the slushy street. "I can't believe the man wants to make a federal case out of this. As if it's so unusual for a fifteen-year-old girl to cut a few classes or smoke a few cigarettes. You wouldn't happen to still have that pack?"

"Huh?"

She looked over at me, then glanced back at the road and slammed on the brakes as we reached an intersection. "I haven't smoked in years, but I wouldn't mind one now."

"I never knew you smoked."

"I started in junior high. But Daddy made such a fuss about it that I finally stopped after we got married, when I was pregnant with you."

I dug through my bag and produced the half-empty pack of cigarettes that I'd bought just last night from the vending machine at Mario's. "So, you want one?" I asked my mother.

"Why not?" I handed one to her and she drove with one hand, swerving and narrowly missing a parked car as she lit up.

I hesitated only a moment before putting a cigarette between my own lips. I glanced at her as I struck the match.

"Go ahead," she said, exhaling a stream of smoke.

"Okay."

She talked a blue streak as she drove toward Peaberry's, which is this café in Bristol that serves gourmet coffee and pastry and stuff. Then she pulled into a parking spot in front of the café, stopping the car with a lurch.

"This is a handicapped spot, Mom," I said.

She shrugged and said in an offhanded way, "So? We won't get caught."

Inside, we ordered large hazelnut coffees. We sat at a booth, sipping and smoking and talking a mile a minute about anything that came to mind, and for once, I was glad *she* was my mother.

When we walked out to the car, there was a parking ticket tucked under the windshield wiper. My mother laughed, ripped it up, and threw the pieces in the air. I cracked up at that. Then we drove straight to the mall, and she bought each of us a new dress to wear on Christmas Day.

And this time, when she said her usual "Don't tell Daddy," it didn't bother me.

We were halfway home before I remembered that I was supposed to be at work.

"Where have you *been?*" asked Margie, the other waitress who was working on my shift as soon as I walked in the door.

"Family crisis," I said vaguely, as my mother had instructed me.

"Wow, is everything all right?"

"Yeah, now it is. My mom said to have Mario call her at home and she'll explain for me."

"Mario's not here yet," Margie said, shoving my apron and nametag into my hands. "And you'd be better off not saying anything to him about being late. Just get busy before he shows up. I've been covering your section."

"Thank you, thank you, thank you, Margie, you're a doll!" I said, rapidly tying the apron on and wincing as I pricked myself with the pin on the nametag.

I grabbed an order pad and scurried into the dining room just as Mario walked in the back door whistling. "Good evening, everyone!" he called cheerfully.

Whew! Close call, I thought as I darted toward the family sitting in the first booth in my section.

12

Wednesday, December 22

It figures that I was almost home free—out of school for Christmas break, that is—when disaster struck.

I guess it really wasn't a disaster, but when I got called out of last period to go down to Miss Rand's office, I knew I wasn't in for a treat.

Miss Rand was waiting for me. She was pretty, with short dark hair, and had on a red sweater with a little Christmas tree-shaped rhinestone pin over her heart. On her desk was a porcelain pot with a pink poinsettia plant. "Karen, have a seat." She smiled and motioned to an overstuffed chair.

I sat on the edge.

"It's been brought to my attention," Miss Rand

said, leaning forward across her desk, "that you cut two classes again yesterday, even after you promised Mr. O'Neill that it wouldn't happen again."

I didn't say anything. My mind darted to the agenda I'd planned for after school. First I was going to buy more wrapping paper—I'd forgotten all about the basketball hoop for Ethan, which was still sitting in the garage. Then I'd stop at the post office to mail the letter I'd written to Sophia. I had to be at Mario's by four, but first I wanted to—

"Karen!" Miss Rand said loudly.

Startled, I looked across at her. "What?"

"Aren't you listening?"

I nodded.

"I don't think you were." She didn't look angry—just concerned. "I was just telling you that over the past week, you've failed tests in every one of your classes and failed to hand in projects in art and social studies. Your teachers are very concerned, and frankly, so am I."

I shrugged.

"Do you have any idea why you might be having trouble with your classes?"

"No."

She went on, not grilling me, just persisting, wanting to know what was going on in my personal life. Was I involved with drugs? Did I have any friends to talk to? Did I feel okay? I didn't answer, just grew more and more agitated, until I got totally fed up.

When Miss Rand asked, for the hundredth time,

"How do you *feel,* Karen?" I jumped up, grabbed her heavy poinsettia plant, and said, "How do I feel? This is how I feel!" Then I dropped it.

The container shattered all over the puky-green tile floor. Clumps of dirt and petals covered my shoes, and I stepped out of the mess, then looked back at Miss Rand.

The expression on her face bothered me. It wasn't that she was mad. Just surprised, and troubled.

"Karen—" she started, but I didn't let her go any further.

"It's none of your business how I feel!" I shouted. "And if you really knew how I felt, you'd just tell me I was crazy!"

I stormed out of her office toward my locker. I thought she might come after me, but she didn't.

I was shaking so hard I almost couldn't do my locker combination. I don't know how I remembered the numbers. I shoved my arms into my jacket sleeves and scooped up my bag, somehow going through the motions. Part of me was acting completely normal, like nothing had happened.

When the principal's voice came over the loudspeaker, the sudden noise made me jump. "I want to wish everyone a happy holiday, and to start off this festive season, I'm going to let you go fifteen minutes early."

I was already running toward the door when the kids came pouring out of their classes. My neighbor

Mike called out my name, but I kept on running, as if I didn't hear him.

When I got home from work that night, I found my mother in the family room, riding her exercise bike and watching *It's a Wonderful Life*.

"Is Daddy home?" I asked.

"Nope. He went to his company Christmas party at the Biltmore in Providence."

"Oh, yeah." I flopped down on the couch. "Weren't you supposed to go with him?"

"I didn't feel like it. Those things are always so dull, and I wasn't in the mood to mingle with all those stuffy people. You hungry? There's pizza in the fridge."

I hadn't been able to eat during my break. I just had a cigarette even though everyone else had ziti and garlic bread.

"I ate at work," I lied. Then I turned up the volume on the TV. It was the scene where George flips out and hollers at his kids and his wife and even at Susu's teacher on the phone.

Seeing good old normal George Bailey out of control on the television screen made me feel instantly better about what had happened in Miss Rand's office today.

"Poor guy," my mother commented as George went storming out into the swirling snow.

"Yeah."

I figured my mother probably related to him, too.

Then I remembered what was coming next.

The part where George stood on the bridge, about to commit suicide.

I couldn't look at my mother. I knew what she was thinking about, though. *Who* she was thinking about.

My aunt Jill.

No one ever mentioned her, though. And we didn't say anything now, either. We just watched the scene in silence.

Then, after Clarence Oddbody, the angel, rescued George and they were in the bar having drinks, my mother suddenly said, "Oh, Karen, I almost forgot!"

"What?"

"I got a phone call this afternoon. From Miss Rand."

"What did she want?" I asked, focusing on the screen.

"She said you cut classes again yesterday and that when she called you down to her office to discuss it, you got a little out of hand. She said you threw a lamp on the floor and that—"

"Not a lamp," I corrected swiftly. "It was a plant."

"A plant. Whatever. She's concerned and thinks you're very troubled about something. She wanted to know if I noticed any changes in your behavior at home lately."

Since I couldn't read my mother's reaction, I had to look over at her. She had slowed her pedaling and was adjusting the controls on her handlebars. She didn't appear to be all that bothered by what Miss Rand had said.

"What'd you tell her?" I asked.

She stopped fiddling with the knobs and started pedaling again. "I told her to mind her own business," she said and laughed.

"You did?"

"No. But I wanted to. I said that you'd been under a lot of pressure lately, trying to juggle schoolwork with your new job and boy troubles."

"Boy troubles? Why do you keep saying that?"

"Why do you think? Because it sounded good. I told Miss Rand that you're going through typical teen ups and downs and not to worry about you."

"What'd she say?"

"That I was probably right and she hadn't realized you were having problems with your boyfriend."

"Way to go, Mom!"

"Karen, forget about this ridiculous school psychologist and old Baldy, too. Don't let them bother you, okay? There's nothing wrong with you."

It was such a relief to have someone say that to me—especially after all the probing Miss Rand had done this afternoon.

13

Friday, December 24

Gina and I both worked on Christmas Eve. Mario was expecting a big crowd, and he was right. Gina and I never got a chance to talk. We were too busy. We'd exchanged gifts just before we left for work. And she'd been thrilled, just as I'd predicted. She had no idea how much the blouse cost, though. She's not really into fashion, like I am. She'd just said, "Karen, you were supposed to stick with our twenty-dollar limit! This must have cost twice that, at least!" And I'd assured her that it didn't matter, saying that I'd gotten it on sale.

She'd bought me a beautiful illustrated hardcover

book about fashion design, and as my dad drove us home, I thanked her for it again. "I can't wait to read it," I told her. "Have fun tonight and tomorrow, and I'll talk to you on Sunday."

"Okay. Merry Christmas. You too, Mr. Spencer."

My dad and I both murmured "Merry Christmas" and watched her go running eagerly through the rain toward the door. The Petrillos' house was all lit up with colored lights, and their tree twinkled merrily in the front window.

As my father backed out of their driveway, then drove toward our own house, I saw that no one had turned on our tree lights or even the glass globe by the front door. Everything was dark except for the window in Ethan's room.

And my mother's car wasn't in the driveway.

"Where did she go?" my father muttered as we pulled in.

"Maybe she ran out to the store for something."

"Everything's closed. It's Christmas Eve."

"The convenience stores are open."

"Yeah," was all he said.

In silence we both walked to the house through the rain that had been steadily falling.

I left my father in the kitchen, went upstairs, and knocked on Ethan's door. Music was blasting from inside, and I had to knock twice more before he called, "Who is it?"

"Karen. Open up."

He did. I saw that he was wearing his uniform of a flannel shirt, baggy pants, and a backward baseball cap.

"Hey," he said.

"Hey. Where's Mom?"

He shrugged.

"You didn't hear her leave?" my father asked, coming up behind me.

"Nope. Why? She isn't here?"

We both shook our heads.

"So? Maybe she went out to the store or something," Ethan said.

"Everything's closed," I told him.

The three of us were silent for a minute.

Then my dad took off his coat and said, "I'm going downstairs to watch TV."

"Should I plug in the Christmas tree?" I asked, for lack of anything else to say.

Dad shrugged. "I don't care."

I thought about it, then shook my head. I decided, Why bother?

I went into my room and changed into pajamas. Then I crawled into bed with the new book from Gina and read until I fell asleep at three in the morning.

My mother still hadn't come home.

Saturday, December 25

It's only a half-hour drive from Valley Cove to my grandparents' house in Newport. All four of us were silent the whole way.

I kept thinking about my mother, and how she'd taken off. I had woken up at six to hear my parents arguing in their bedroom. My father was demanding to know where my mother had been all night, and she'd told him she went to a homeless shelter to sing carols and "spread Christmas cheer to people who need it." My father had acted as if he didn't believe her, but knowing my mother, it was probably true. Just last summer I saw her hand a bag lady two hundred dollars.

I had gone back to sleep, afraid that when I woke up, she would have taken off again. But when Ethan and I got up later, she was there, drinking coffee in the kitchen.

We'd gone through the motions of Christmas morning, plugging in the tree, and sitting in the living room, opening gifts. Mostly all we said was "This one is for you," or "Thanks, this is really nice," or whatever.

My mother did smile when she opened the earrings I'd bought her, though. And I know Ethan was psyched about the basketball hoop. My father tried to act as if he was glad to get the tennis racket I'd bought him, although I could tell he was wondering what he was going to do with it, since he didn't play tennis.

My grandparents' house was a small bungalow on a cramped side street, the only one on the block with no outside decorations or lights. Inside, we found my grandfather in the living room, watching television with the sound blasting. He's usually pretty quiet, unless he's angry about something.

"Hi, Dad, Merry Christmas," my mother said, bending down to give him a kiss.

He handed Ethan and me each a twenty-dollar bill and said, "Here. Merry Christmas." He did that every year.

My mother had disappeared into the kitchen.

The three of us followed her and found her leaning sullenly against the counter while my grandmother took something out of the oven. Grandma was kind of put out because we were late, and she's a real stickler for punctuality.

But she was happy to see us. She told me she liked my haircut and said she couldn't believe how tall Ethan was getting.

A few minutes later we all sat down in the dining room to eat. The meal was predictably dull, at first.

Then it happened.

It was my father who slipped and mentioned my aunt Jill, my mother's younger sister.

He was in the middle of some drawn-out story about a past Christmas, and I was wondering why he was even making an effort to keep conversation flowing, when he said, "And then Jill insisted on going out sledding . . ."

He trailed off when he realized what he'd done.

My grandparents never, ever talk about my aunt. As soon as they heard her name, they both stopped eating and just sat staring at their plates.

My mother shot my father a furious look, as if to say, *Now see what you've done!*

He just shrugged, frowned back at her, and hastily finished, "Anyway, that was some storm that year. I don't think we've had that much snow since." Then he picked up his glass and took a big swallow of water.

My grandmother cleared her throat and said, "Would anyone like some more potatoes? There are plenty left."

We all murmured no thanks, we were fine.

"You want to go down to the water?" Ethan asked as we stood on the street outside our grandparents' house. We had managed to escape, saying we needed to go for a walk to get some exercise after that huge meal.

I finished buttoning up my coat and looked around. The street was gray and misty and deserted. "Why not?" I said. "We've got a couple hours to kill."

I noticed that nearly every house we passed was all lit up with Christmas decorations, even though it was just the middle of the afternoon.

Ethan and I didn't say much as we walked. When we

reached the deserted waterfront, we passed closed shops and a baseball diamond, then headed for the park along one side of the harbor. The greenish water was pretty choppy.

"It's starting to get pretty foggy," Ethan said. We both glanced off in the distance at the enormous Newport Bridge. It spanned two miles to Conanicut Island.

"I can't believe she actually tried to jump off that thing," Ethan said, voicing my own thoughts. He plopped down on a bench facing the bridge.

I sat next to him. "I know. She was just a little older than me when she did it. I wonder if she really wanted to kill herself."

"She," of course, was Aunt Jill.

"Who knows? If that guy hadn't driven by, seen her on the edge, and called the cops, who knows what would have happened?"

"You know what I've always wondered? Whether anyone called Grandpa and Grandma. I wonder if they were here, trying to talk her down."

I knew there was a huge commotion that day, with a big crowd gathered, watching.

"Does anyone bring it up to you these days?" I asked him.

"Once Dad said something about her. I think he said she was 'nutty.'"

Years ago I had asked about her, and my father had told me she was always running away and throwing tantrums. And she was an alcoholic.

My brother and I had only seen her a handful of times in our whole lives. That was when we were much younger, when my aunt was out of the hospital and living with my grandparents for a while when she was about twenty-one.

"Do you remember her, Eth?" I asked because he's a year and a half younger than me.

"Not much. She had long, straight brown hair, right?"

I nodded. If there were pictures of Aunt Jill at my grandparents' house or at ours, they were hidden away. But I vaguely recalled her hair, too, and that she was really skinny.

"I remember the way she talked, too," Ethan said. "A mile a minute and kind of high pitched."

"Yeah, I know." For a moment I was silent, lost in my memories. Then I said, "You know, I always thought she was a lot of fun. She'd laugh a lot and get down on the floor and crawl around."

"Yeah, and we used to play jungle with her, and she'd do that Tarzan yell and Grandpa would yell at her to shut up." Ethan shook his head. "You know what else I remember? That her breath always smelled kind of mediciney, like cough syrup."

"That was the liquor, Eth."

"I know. Where do you think she is now, Karen?"

"A long time ago I overheard Grandma say something about how she's in a halfway house near Boston because she isn't capable of taking care of herself anymore."

"Yeah, well, knowing them, they probably just didn't want to deal with her," Ethan said bluntly.

"Yeah, it was probably too much of an embarrassment. A nutcase in the family." My grandparents have always been really concerned about what people think.

"You want to go back?" Ethan asked.

"Not really, but I guess we have to," I said.

And together, my brother and I headed away from the water and the bridge.

14

Tuesday, December 28

I spent the next two days in my room, sleeping and moping around. Post-holiday letdown, I guessed. Besides, the weather had been gray and mostly sleeting. I wasn't the only one who was out of it. My mother had been in bed ever since Christmas night, claiming she was run-down and needed to rest. I finally got a rush of energy and called the Petrillos' to see if Gina wanted to go skating. But Gina had strep throat. I suddenly felt as if I'd burst if I didn't get out and do something.

Luckily my friend Mike was just hanging out at his house, so he said he'd go with me. With my skates slung over my shoulder, I stopped to pick him up, and we headed over to Bayview Park. It was one of those brilliant winter days, when the cold air was invigorating. I watched my breath come out in quick *whooshes* as I bounced along.

"What's your rush?" Mike said. "Save some of your energy for the ice."

"Come on," I said, pulling him by the sleeve as we entered the park. "Let's get out there."

As soon as we got to the edge of the pond, I saw Matt. He was wearing a hunter-green down ski jacket and black jeans, and he was skating with some blond girl in a cheerleader's jacket from St. Isabel's, a Catholic high school in Providence.

I kept an eye on them as Mike and I sat on a little wooden bench and laced up our skates. I know Matt spotted me as he went by, because he almost bumped into someone head-on.

I found myself feeling pleased that he was distracted by my presence—especially when he was with another girl.

"What's Matt doing with that girl?" I asked. "Who is she?"

"Her name's Maureen Riley," Mike said, standing up tentatively on his blades. "She's a cheerleader at St. Isabel's."

He wobbled over to the edge of the pond and stepped onto the ice. Turning, he put his hands on his hips and said, "You're the one who was in the big rush to skate. Let's go!"

But I just sat there on the bench, in the middle of doing up my second skate, and watched Matt. Matt and Maureen. Matt coming to a quick stop on the edge of his blades and throwing up a tail of shaved ice. Maureen letting out a *whoop* and skating right into him. Maureen falling down and Matt giving her his hand to help her up.

That should be me, I thought, *holding his warm hand.*

"Earth to Karen, do you read me?"

I blinked and looked up at Mike, who threw a little snowball at me.

"How long have they been going out?" I asked. I wondered if it was possible that Matt had been interested in Maureen even while he was taking me out.

"A little longer than a week, I guess," Mike said.

As I skated onto the ice, I continued to watch Matt and Maureen. Matt didn't look at me, though. I wished he would.

Normally I was cautious when it came to skating. I could do a few tricks, but rarely tried them.

But today I was fearless and totally confident. I tried to skate closer to Matt, just close enough so he'd see me, without my being too obvious. I glided smoothly around the pond, doing jumps and spins and weaving skillfully in and out of the other skaters. And I'm sure that Matt was watching me.

At one point Mike caught up with me and said breathlessly, "Karen, what are you doing?"

"What do you mean?" I asked, pushing off effortlessly alongside him.

"I mean, who do you think you are? What's with the show you're putting on?"

"I'm not putting on a show!" Irritated, I skated away from him. I found myself about ten feet behind Matt and Maureen, and I continued skating behind them as they circled the pond. I imagined how it would be to skate up to Matt—if he were alone—and tuck my arm under his. We could share each other's warmth and skate in unison. We'd make a perfect couple, much better than he and Maureen. He was probably only going out with her because he was on the rebound, I figured. I was sure I could get him away from her if I tried.

And that's what I decided to do. I would get him back. We belonged together. He was the only guy who could really understand me, and I could make him happy.

I watched Matt and Maureen skate off the ice and take off their skates and then trudge through the snow and out of the park. As Matt's green coat disappeared down the street, I knew what I had to do.

A few minutes later Mike gave me the perfect opportunity to put my plan into action. As we unlaced our skates he asked, "Are you going to Lucas Marshall's party on New Year's Eve?"

I had been in my own little world for so long that I hadn't heard anything about it. "Who's going?" I asked, my mind racing.

"Oh, you know, whoever shows up. Lucas passed the word around that anybody could come—his parents will be away."

"Is Matt going?" I asked.

"Yeah, I think so."

This is going to be the best thing that ever happened to me, I thought as we left the park. New Year's Eve would be the perfect night for Matt and me to get together again. It was the most romantic night of the year.

It wasn't until I reached my house that I remembered I was supposed to work New Year's Eve. There was no way I was going to miss Lucas's party, so there was only one thing to do.

I'd just call in sick.

107

15

Friday, December 31

At eight o'clock on New Year's Eve I checked myself out in the bedroom mirror one last time. I was wearing a skimpy black minidress and new black patent heels I'd bought at the mall the day before. I'd also bought some black lace panty hose—something no St. Isabel's cheerleader would ever wear.

For the past few hours I had been playing the same song over and over on my stereo. It was by U2, called "All I Need Is You," and Matt and I had slow-danced to it at the Winter Gala. I hadn't listened to the whole CD yet because I didn't really care about any of the other songs.

I decided that "All I Need Is You" should be our

song, mine and Matt's. That's not all I decided. Matt and I would be together for the rest of our lives. I just knew it. And I had big plans for us. We would move to New York together right after graduation, and he'd become an author and I'd become a fashion designer. And I had the greatest idea for what we could name our first-born child, which I was positive was going to be a girl. "Maren"—a combination of "Matt" and "Karen"! I couldn't wait to tell Matt about it.

And I was dying to tell Gina, too. I hadn't spoken to her all week, which was probably a good thing. She would kill me if she found out I had called in sick tonight. Not that she'd ever find out what I was really doing. I planned to tell everyone at the party to keep their mouths shut about seeing me there.

I got closer to the mirror and studied my makeup. Eyeliner and lipstick—just right. I put on a little more blush. My hair looked terrific, for once, glossy and smooth, with just the right amount of wave. I was wearing new gold dangle earrings that had just arrived from the home-shopping order I'd placed.

I guessed my parents hadn't gotten their Visa bill yet, because no one had asked me about the charges I'd made. I hoped it wouldn't come for another few days, because I was pretty broke. I'd spent all my money at the mall on the dress and CDs. In fact, I had to take another hundred out of my savings account when I found the perfect shoes and panty hose to go with the dress.

I turned away from the mirror, feeling giddy with

excitement. It was time to leave. Matt would probably be there already. I was going to walk over to the party, which was only a few blocks away.

I went downstairs and put on my coat. No one was home. Ethan was at a movie with his friends. My parents had left around five for some party in Cranston. My father practically had to drag my mother out of bed and force her to go, and she had cried the whole time she was getting ready. What a nut.

When I got to the party, the first thing I did was look around for Matt. The house was crowded and noisy, with the stereo competing with the TV. I rushed through each room searching for him, ignoring everyone who said hi to me. When I spotted Mike, I rushed over to him.

"Karen—wow!" Mike said. "You're looking—"

"Have you seen Matt? Is he here yet?" I asked Mike before he could finish his sentence.

"Haven't seen him," Mike answered. "You look great, Karen."

I took a big breath and said thanks, my eyes darting around the room. What if he didn't come? My heart was racing.

Mike was asking me what Ethan was doing for New Year's, and I answered with a shrug, "Out with his friends somewhere."

Mike wandered into the living room, where most of the guys were huddled around the TV, watching some sports bloopers show. I went into the bathroom and checked out my hair and touched up my lipstick. I tried to calm myself, telling myself Matt would show up, that this was the biggest party happening tonight, and that all his friends would be here. As I was adjusting my panty hose, someone knocked on the door and told me to hurry up. Feeling flustered, I walked out of the bathroom and through the kitchen toward the living room. Just as I reached the living room, the front door opened and Matt walked in, with Maureen.

I stood behind a few kids so I could watch him for a minute before he saw me. And the first thing I noticed was that Matt was holding Maureen's hand. He was smiling, and his cheeks were flushed from the cold. He looked really glad to see everyone at the party and grabbed one of his friends by the shoulder to say hello. His eyes darted around the room until they came to rest on me. And then his expression changed suddenly, and he didn't seem so happy anymore. His smile disappeared, and he just nodded once. I smiled at him as brightly as I could and said hi. But by the time the word was out of my mouth, he had turned to ask Maureen a question.

I watched as Matt and Maureen moved closer to the TV. When someone got up out of a big overstuffed chair, Matt sat down in it and pulled Maureen down to sit on the arm of the chair. They didn't stop holding hands the whole time. I stood against the wall and quietly watched them.

Maureen seemed to know all about football, since

she was a cheerleader, I guess. I studied her outfit, noticing how nice her blond hair looked against her dark blue velvet dress. At one point Maureen leaned down and whispered something in Matt's ear. He brushed her hair away as she spoke.

I decided I couldn't just stand there and hope Matt would notice me; I'd have to get closer to him and start up a conversation. I took the next chair that was empty and tried to act like I was interested in what was on TV. I had no idea what was going on, what was so funny, but I laughed every time Lucas and the other guys whooped and hollered.

I heard Matt ask Maureen if she wanted something to drink, and she nodded. Matt got up and walked into the kitchen, while Maureen waited for him on the arm of the chair. Now was my chance.

Matt was talking to Candace Meyers in the kitchen by the punch bowl, and I had to push through a crowd of people to get closer to him. Someone shouted out "Excuse me" in a nasty tone as I brushed by, but I didn't turn to see who it was. My eyes were on Matt's wavy brown hair.

"So, Matt," I said, interrupting his conversation with Candace, "how'd you like the skating the other day?"

Matt didn't seem to hear me. He just glanced at me and continued talking.

"Matt?" I said again, and he turned to me with a puzzled expression.

"What did you say?" he asked with a slight frown.

I decided to be more direct. "I was wondering if you wanted to go skating with me sometime. Maybe tomorrow, at the park."

He just stared into my eyes for a few seconds, almost as if he didn't understand the question. Then he slowly said, "I don't think so."

I stood still and watched him walk away, with two glasses of punch in his hands. I was vaguely aware of all the noise and activity around me. Then Lucas was next to me, saying, "Don't hog all the punch for yourself, Karen. Save some for me." I didn't even look at him as I made my way back into the living room.

Matt and Maureen were standing to my right as I walked into the room. I stood next to them and drank some punch, determined to try again. Matt didn't even know I was there. He was talking to Maureen and laughing about something. I had to try again.

I touched him lightly on the arm and said, "Matt?"

He and Maureen both turned to me. "Matt, I need to talk to you for a minute. Alone."

Matt acted as if he couldn't believe he'd heard right. Then he said in a low, quiet voice, "Karen. I'm with Maureen."

"But Matt," I said, "we need to talk. We *have* to talk."

Matt put his arm around Maureen and walked her into the kitchen.

I hadn't given any thought to what to do if my plan

didn't work. I'd planned on leaving the party with Matt and going back to my parents' house, where we could be alone with each other. I thought we would walk through the crystal-clear night holding hands, and when we got to my parents' house, we'd watch the ball go down at Times Square on TV, and we'd kiss at midnight.

But Matt wouldn't talk to me; he'd barely even look at me. I couldn't believe it was happening. Did he really care about her? He couldn't possibly care about Little Miss Cheerleader. I would have to ask him if he was going out with her to make me jealous. And I would tell him that I understood, and that I wasn't mad, and that we belonged together. I walked into the kitchen but didn't find him anywhere. I kept searching, through the dining room and into the den. The room was quiet, and there didn't seem to be anyone in there when I peeked inside.

But then I saw that I was wrong. Matt was in the den. I heard his voice, then I heard Maureen laugh softly. I stepped into the room and stood frozen as I saw what they were doing. They were on the couch with their arms around each other, kissing. Matt was kissing Maureen in the way I'd dreamed he'd kiss me.

Matt didn't know that I'd seen them, or that I left the room fighting back tears. He didn't know that after I got my coat and sneaked out the back door, I walked home alone on New Year's Eve, tears streaming down my face.

Saturday, January 1

"Karen?"

The voice startled me out of a dead sleep.

Confused, I rolled over and looked around.

Gina was standing in the doorway of my room, wearing a coat and scarf.

"What are you doing here?" I asked, blinking. What was going on?

Then it started coming back to me. I closed my eyes. Oh, God.

Last night . . . New Year's Eve . . . *Matt.*

The last thing I remembered was throwing myself, sobbing, onto my bed.

"Your brother let me in," Gina said, taking a few steps closer to my bed.

I opened my eyes and looked up at her again. That was when I saw her grim expression. Her eyes didn't have their usual sparkle, probably from being sick.

And their expression was cold.

"Why are you looking at me like that?" I asked her, frowning. "And why aren't you home in bed? I thought you were sick."

"Yeah, and I thought *you* were sick, too."

Uh-oh.

"I *am* sick," I said, coughing and burrowing into the blankets.

"Oh, yeah, right," she said in this really sarcastic

tone. "You're real sick. My uncle was left so short-handed, he had to call me and beg me to come in. And since I was feeling better, I went. And I actually felt sorry for you, Karen. I was worried that you'd caught strep from me or something."

"I think I might have," I said, clearing my throat really loud.

"Yeah, right. You have strep throat. That's why you were at Lucas Marshall's party last night."

"I was not!" I blurted out.

"You were *so!* Candace and Teddy and a bunch of other people came in for pizza after midnight. I waited on them, and they told me you were there. And I was like, *'Karen* was at the party tonight? *Karen Spencer?'* And they said yes. And my uncle Mario had come up behind me, and he heard the whole thing. He said you're fired. And you know what, Karen? I'm *glad!'*

She looked so unlike herself, so furious. I closed my eyes so I wouldn't have to see her face.

But she kept right on talking. "You know what, Karen? When they first said it was you at the party, I didn't believe it. I mean, I kept arguing with Teddy, saying, 'Karen wouldn't do something like that. She wouldn't call in sick to work and then go off to a party.' He must have thought I was such an idiot, Karen!"

I didn't say anything to that, just turned away from her. "Why don't you get out of here?" I asked, closing my eyes.

"Because I think you should apologize to me, Karen. I got you that job, even though I knew you were going to screw it up. You *promised* me you wouldn't, and I told myself I should believe you, because you're my best friend—I mean, you *were* my best friend. But I don't want to hang around with someone who lies. Someone who's totally irresponsible. Someone who's—*crazy!*"

When she flung that last word at me, it was all I could take.

I sat up, whirled around, and screamed at her, "Get out!"

She stared at me for a second, then turned and headed for the door. "Gladly," was all she said before she slammed it behind her.

Wednesday, January 5

I had spent the last three days at home, in bed, crying and sleeping and staring at the ceiling. I'd told my mother I was sick, and she'd written a note for me to bring back to school to explain my absence.

It had been torture to drag myself out of bed and get ready for school. I kept telling myself that the walk through the icy January morning would make me feel better—or at least more awake—but it didn't help much.

As I plodded along the sidewalk, I struggled not to cry. I was upset about what had happened at the party with Matt, but even more upset about my fight with

Gina. She was supposed to be my best friend, and she'd actually accused me of being crazy. That, I couldn't handle.

At school I dumped my stuff in my locker, wiping away the tears that kept slipping from my eyes, and went into homeroom.

I was half aware that Matt was there, and that he kept his back to me the whole time. But I didn't care, not really. Not about him, and not, I decided, about Gina, either. I avoided her all day.

All I wanted to do was go back to bed. That was exactly what I did as soon as I got home.

I was in my room, sleeping, when the door burst open and my mother was suddenly there.

"Karen, it's time to eat. And we're having a special dinner. Come on, aren't you hungry?"

My mind wandered back to what I'd eaten in the past few days. Not much. A few bagels here and there, and some soda or juice on the few occasions I'd managed to get out of bed.

My mother pulled back the covers and said, "Come on, right now. Ethan's home, and he's waiting at the table."

I sighed and got up. In the kitchen I found a mess. There were pots and pans and bowls and spills and open cans and packages of food everywhere.

Obviously, my mother had cooked. Chattering a mile a minute about how important it was to get proper nutrition, she started slopping stuff on our plates—meat loaf and baked chicken and mashed potatoes and gravy and corn bread and macaroni and cheese and different kinds of vegetables.

"How come you made all this stuff, Ma?" Ethan asked, eyeing the piles of food in front of him.

She snapped, "What do you mean, how come? Are you accusing me of being a bad mother? Do I normally not feed you enough? Are you starving? Are you malnourished? Are you—"

"Geez, calm down. I just meant—I mean, meat loaf *and* chicken?"

"Ethan, if you don't want it, don't eat it!" she said shrilly.

"I want it; I want it," he said and grimly started shoveling it in.

Ethan was the only one who ate, though. My mother, for all her talk about the wonderful meal in front of us, just drank one cup of coffee after another without touching her food. I picked at mine, but it was just too much effort to eat much of it. The fork seemed incredibly heavy, for some reason, and I was exhausted from chewing and swallowing after the first few minutes. But I kept trying, because the last thing I wanted was for my mother to erupt into a tantrum.

She started in on how demanding my father's company was. He had to leave the next day for a sales conference in Florida. How did they expect him to have any kind of family life? she was saying when the phone rang. She jumped up so fast to answer it that she knocked her chair over.

"Oh, hi, Sandy!" she said into the phone. She took

the phone, which was cordless, into the other room to talk. Ethan and I heard her go into the den, still chattering, and then we heard her get on her exercise bike and start pedaling.

Ethan got up, picked up the chair my mother had toppled over, and looked at me. "Karen, what's with her? I mean, do you think Mom's—crazy?"

"You mean you think so, too?" Relief flooded in. So it wasn't me. It was my mother.

"Yeah."

I opened my mouth to say more but suddenly felt as if I was going to start crying, so I closed it again.

"Karen," Ethan said, watching me. "Are you all right?"

I nodded.

"What's wrong?"

"Nothing." I stared at my still-loaded plate.

"You sure?"

"I had a fight with Gina," I murmured.

Ethan seemed relieved. "So that's it. I knew something was up. Do you, uh, want to talk about it or something?"

I shook my head.

"Okay." He reached over and turned on the television. A sportscaster was talking about some basketball player who'd injured his ankle, and Ethan immediately turned up the volume and zeroed in on it.

He didn't even notice that I'd started to cry. Tears sliding down my face, I slipped away and went back up to my room.

16

Friday, January 7

Finally things were starting to get back to normal. At least I'd stopped crying constantly, and I hadn't been sleeping as much. I felt better, except that things with Gina hadn't changed. We still weren't speaking. She'd been eating lunch with Teddy every day, and I guess she was all wrapped up in him now. I ignored the two of them when I was in the cafeteria. I just sat alone at a table and read while I ate.

Matt was still ignoring me, and I was actually glad, because I couldn't deal with him. In biology we didn't speak at all, and luckily we weren't going to start animal dissections for another few weeks, so we could keep our distance.

Even when I overheard Candace Meyers asking him about Maureen, and Matt saying yes, he was still dating her, it didn't bother me.

After school I went straight home. I was sitting in the kitchen, flipping the pages of a *Vogue* magazine, and doodling on the back of a notebook, when the phone rang.

"Karen? It's Dad," my father said when I answered.

"How's Florida?"

"Fine. Karen, did you give your access code for your savings account to anyone?"

Uh-oh.

"No," I said and started chewing on my lower lip.

"Did you write it down someplace, then, where someone could have seen it?"

"Uh-uh."

There was a long pause. Then he said, "I knew it."

"Knew what, Dad?"

He paused. "Karen, I was looking over some bank statements while I was on the plane and saw that someone has been taking money out of your account. And I think I know who that someone is."

So I'd been nabbed. "I meant to put the money back, Dad, I swear," I said in a rush. "I was going to—"

"You made the withdrawals?"

I blinked. "Yeah. Why? Who did you . . ." I trailed off as it dawned on me.

He'd actually thought my mother was taking money out of my account. I couldn't believe it. I mean, I knew my mother was terrible when it came to money, but she wouldn't actually *steal* from her kids!

"Karen, why did you take that money out?" my father asked evenly.

I hesitated. "Christmas presents."

There was a long pause. Then he said in a deadly quiet voice, "I see."

"But I meant to put it back."

"And why haven't you?"

"Because . . ." I hadn't told my parents I'd been fired from Mario's. Neither of them noticed that I wasn't working, my father because he was never home, and my mother because, well, she was just totally out of it these days.

"I'm sorry," was all I said. I hung up and looked at the phone for a minute. Then I shrugged and said, "Who cares?"

Sunday, January 9

I had been in bed since Friday night. When I wasn't sleeping, I was crying. At least no one was bugging me. My father was still in Florida, my brother was at a basketball tournament in Hartford, and who knew what my mother was up to.

Finally, on Sunday, I got out of bed and went over to my desk. I felt like drawing, so I took out my sketchpad and started copying a still-life I'd ripped out of a magazine a few weeks ago.

My charcoal strokes were too heavy and jagged, though, and no matter how I tried, I couldn't get it right. I kept ripping up page after page, tossing the pieces onto the floor beside my chair.

Finally, in frustration, I put away the sketchpad and took the spiral-bound notebook off my bookshelf. I had decorated the cover a year ago, with flowers and rainbows and big puffy clouds. In the center, in swirly pink lettering, it said, "Poems by Karen Spencer."

I sat down at my desk and started flipping through it. The first few poems, like the cover, were upbeat and light. But as I turned the pages, I saw that my poetry had become increasingly dark and heavy, full of depressing, even violent images. I realized that these days, I only wrote when I was feeling down.

When I came to the first blank page, I picked up a pen and stared at it for a long time. Then I scribbled the first few lines of a new poem.

> Trapped in this cold, bleak world,
> I watch, helpless,
> as relentless winter days
> march cruelly on,
> like Nazis . . .
> like death.

17

Thursday, January 13

For the first time since before Christmas, I cut three classes. This time I slipped out the back door in the A building and walked out across the foggy football field. It was drizzling out and my boots were full of mud, but I didn't care. I just kept plodding along aimlessly, my hands jammed into the pockets of my jeans and my backpack slung over my shoulder, until I reached the woods beyond the field.

It was quiet among the trees, and the rain made a sifting sound as it fell. It was kind of soothing. I reached the creek that trickled through a field and then into more woods that were at the end of our street. Gina and I used to play by that part of the creek. There was a big rock we used to sit on, pretending we were guarding a priceless treasure from imaginary bad guys who were trying to get it.

Thinking about Gina as I walked in the woods, I started to cry. For the first time I really missed her. Even if she didn't understand me, she was my friend and I knew she cared about me. Not anymore, though. Whenever I caught her looking at me in school, I couldn't read the expression on her face, but it wasn't kind or warm or friendly.

I missed my father, too. He'd come back from Florida earlier in the week but had left on another business trip this morning.

And I missed my mother. I started crying harder when I thought about her. She wasn't a perfect mother—far from it—but at least there were times when she acted normal. Now she was always either moping in her room or ready to scream at us for no reason at all.

I needed her. I remembered how, when I was really little and I'd had a nightmare or had a stomachache, she'd come and sit on my bed in the middle of the night and make me feel better.

I needed her to be there for me now, to tell me not to worry about the mess I'd made of my life. I needed her to protect me from the shapeless, faceless, horrible black thing that seemed to be lurking somewhere, ready to swallow me up.

Before I realized how far I'd gone, I'd reached the

big rock Gina and I used to play on. The rock was sheltered in some pine trees, and I almost walked right by it. I was tired and wet, so I sat down, and the trees kept most of the rain off me. Looking around, I realized that the trees hadn't been so big the last time I was here, which was years ago. The rock was almost engulfed in the overgrowth now.

Rummaging through my backpack, I found my cigarettes, then had to empty everything out of the pack and onto the rock to find a match.

I lit the cigarette and threw the match down on the flat rock. I stared blankly out into the gray day as I smoked, and then I noticed the smell of something burning. Looking down, I saw that I'd thrown the lit match on my sketchpad. In the pad were some charcoal sketches I'd attempted over the weekend and some portraits I'd been working on in art class.

I watched a corner of the paper curl up and blacken as it burned. The smoke stung my eyes and drew more tears. I brushed them away and continued to watch the sketchpad burn.

The drizzle was preventing the fire from burning the pad completely, so I had to help it along. I lit another match and started a flame on the other corner of the pad, blowing on it to keep it lit.

Soon the whole pad had turned to ashes.

When I got to art class, I sat in a corner so that Mrs. Rosenbaum wouldn't see that I didn't have my sketchpad and couldn't finish my project. I'd been staring at a sheet of blank white paper that I borrowed from somebody when an office messenger showed up.

As soon as I saw him hand a note to Mrs. Rosenbaum, I knew what it was about.

I saw her glance at me in a concerned, hesitant way when she handed me the note, as if she wanted to ask me something. I just brushed by her.

When I got into the hall, I glanced at the slip of paper, even though I knew it was a summons to O'Neill's office again, for cutting this morning.

But I was wrong.

It was a summons to Miss Rand's office.

I stared at it for a long time.

Then I tossed it into a trash bin, went to my locker, took out my coat, and left school without a backward glance.

The house was empty when I got there. By that time I was crying really hard.

I didn't know what to do. I was going to be in big trouble at school whenever I went back. I couldn't avoid it forever.

Sooner or later I'd have to face Miss Rand. And I'd have to face everything else in my life, which was falling apart.

My grades—every single one of them was failing.

And Matt was looking at me this morning with a mixture of anger and pity in his eyes.

And Gina, who hated me and had a right to.

How was I going to deal with everything? It was overwhelming.

I can't. I can't handle it, I moaned to myself.

I stood in the upstairs hallway, in so much emotional pain that I couldn't stand it.

I had to escape somehow.

I had to find a place where I could be alone.

I thought briefly about running away.

No. I couldn't do that.

I didn't have the energy.

All I wanted to do was roll up in a little ball and lie down someplace and go to sleep.

The problem was, I always woke up. And when I did, nothing would be better.

With my eyes filled with tears, I moved blindly along the hallway, toward the closed door at the end.

I opened it and walked into my parents' room.

"Please . . ." I moaned. "Please, I need to get away. It hurts so bad—I just need to get away."

I went into my parents' bathroom and studied my face for a moment in the mirrored cabinet over the sink. My eyes had dark shadows under them, and my face was gaunt.

I shook my head in despair, reached out, and opened the cabinet.

There.

The little transparent orange bottles were still there.

And among them, I found what I was looking for.

I was so relieved that I burst into fresh tears. I

opened the bottle and held it over my trembling, outstretched palm.

I shook a few of the little white pills into it.

Then a few more.

And then I emptied the rest of the bottle into my hand, brought it up to my mouth, and started swallowing.

18

Friday, January 14

I opened my eyes and then immediately closed them again. It was too bright—why was everything so bright? Where was I?

Oh, my God . . . am I in Heaven?

I waited a moment, then tried again. Slowly I lifted my eyelids and saw that I was in a white room with a huge window, and it was snowing, hard, beyond the glass. *No wonder,* I told myself, vaguely relieved. And then I realized that I still didn't know where I was or what was going on.

I moved my head, trying to lift it, but it was too heavy. Instantly, though, as soon as I moved, I heard a scrambling sound nearby.

"Karen? Are you awake?"

Then my mother was directly in my field of vision, her face about two inches from mine. I frowned at her. What was she doing here? What was I doing here? Where was *here?*

"Where—" I began, but my voice came out in a croak.

"The hospital," she said quietly. "Do you remember what happened?"

"No . . ."

Yes. I did. I knew what had happened. I had taken too many sleeping pills. I closed my eyes again.

"Karen, wait. Stay awake, Okay? Stay awake and talk to me, Karen." I realized she was squeezing my hand, that she had been holding it all along, even before I woke up.

I looked at her again.

"Karen, if I hadn't come home when I did yesterday afternoon—if I hadn't happened to go into the bathroom to put away the new towels I'd just bought . . ." She shook her head. "Thank God I found you."

"Yesterday?" was all I said.

She nodded. "You've been out for a long time. It's morning."

"My throat—"

"Hurts." She nodded. "The doctors gave you something to make you vomit. You brought up most of the pills. I drove you to the hospital myself. I didn't call an ambulance, Karen, because I knew you wouldn't have wanted the whole neighborhood to know what happened."

I just looked at her fuzzily.

"And we don't have to tell Daddy, okay? Or Ethan," she went on. "This will be our secret. The hospital people have been very nice to me. They told me that our insurance will cover everything, and that they don't need to contact Daddy. I'll make sure he doesn't see the insurance claim when it comes in the mail."

What was she going on and on about? I was too drained to listen. I started to slip into unconsciousness again, but she was still talking, asking me something.

"What?" I finally asked wearily.

"I just wanted to know why. Why did you do it, Karen?"

I tried to shrug, but I couldn't seem to move my shoulders, so I finally said, "I don't know why, Mommy."

I hadn't called her that in years.

Before I let my eyes drift closed again, I saw that there were tears in her eyes. "It's all right, Karen. I'm here. I'm right here. You'll be all right," she whispered.

And I wanted to believe her. I wanted her to make it all go away—my fear, the empty feeling, the confusion, the tears—just like she'd made it go away years ago.

* * *

"How are you, Karen? I'm Dr. Duffy, and I'm a psychiatrist. Your mother is waiting down the hall while I talk to you."

I just stared at him.

He started talking, asking me questions. Just like Miss Rand had. And like the other person who'd visited me earlier today had done. I hadn't talked to her, either, and she hadn't pushed me.

Dr. Duffy kept talking, unfazed that I wasn't answering anything he asked me. Finally, though, he said something that made my heart do a little flip-flop and my hands clench the sheet more tightly.

"Karen, your mother told me your aunt suffers from manic-depressive illness. Were you unaware of her condition?"

"I just—I thought she was an alcoholic," I muttered.

"According to your mother, she is unable to care for herself and has been in a residential treatment program in Boston for several years now."

"My *mother* told you all this?"

He nodded.

"So? What does that have to do with *me?*"

Gina's words, and Matt's, came rushing back to haunt me.

You're crazy, Karen.

Dr. Duffy pulled his chair closer to my bed. "I'm not sure that it has anything to do with you. That's what I'm trying to find out. Do you know what manic-depressive illness is, Karen?"

"No."

"It's a chemical imbalance in the brain, and it causes episodes of mania, or 'highs,' and depression, or 'lows.'"

I didn't answer him.

"Karen," he asked, "do you ever have days when you feel really down and depressed?"

"Doesn't everyone?"

"What do you do when you feel that way?"

"I just—I stay in bed and sleep. And I cry. You know—what anyone does when they're depressed," I said impatiently.

"How long do those times last?"

"I don't know, a few days—"

"You stay in bed for several days at a time?"

The way he asked that made me not want to answer. I just stared him in the eye and said, "Look, everyone has mood swings. I'm not any different. And I'm definitely not crazy."

"No one accused you of being crazy, Karen."

That showed what he knew.

"And you're right," he went on. "Everyone has mood swings now and then. But people who suffer from a depressive disorder experience extremes. They can have very sad periods. Or they can have trouble sleeping. Or they can cry a lot."

"Oh."

"There can be a loss of appetite. Or they can lose interest in the things they usually care about."

"Oh," I said again and turned away from his probing stare.

"Karen," he said gently, "do you think that you may have experienced some of the things we've talked about?"

"No!" I said directly to him. "Why? Do you think that just because my aunt is a nutcase, I am, too?"

"You are not a 'nutcase,' as you put it, Karen. But you may have a biochemical illness that can be treated. There are drugs that can do wonders for people suffering from depression."

"Can you please get my mother so that I can go home now?"

"You can go home tomorrow, Karen. But you are going to be required to attend mandatory counseling sessions so that—"

"No way!" I cut in angrily.

"So that we can get to the bottom of your problem and help you to get it under control."

"No way!" I said again, scowling at him. "I don't have a problem."

He didn't say anything more about it, though. He just started talking in that soothing voice of his again, asking me more questions. I tuned him out until he finally got up and left.

19

Saturday, January 15

Who do they think they are, telling us what to do? Your father doesn't have time for this!" my mother hollered, banging the steering wheel. She was driving me home from the hospital, raving about how we were supposed to go to some mandatory family counseling session, all of us, this coming weekend. "And Ethan has nothing to do with any of this. For God's sake, I told him you were in the hospital because you'd slipped on the ice and hurt your back. Now I'm going to go home and tell him you tried to kill yourself, and he has to give up his basketball game on Saturday night to go talk to a shrink?"

"Look out!" I said, and she swerved in time to miss a car that was stopped to make a left-hand turn.

"And what about me? Do *I* need to go to some wacko shrink? Do they think I'm not a good mother? Is that what this is about?"

"No, Mom," I said, laying a hand on her sleeve. My eyes were all teary, but I didn't want to start crying because I was afraid I'd never stop.

"Karen, baby, don't you worry about any of this. They can't force us to go to these things. I mean, what are they going to do, come and drag us out of the house? We'll just forget about this whole thing and get back to normal."

"But what about—"

"Karen, I said don't worry! Nobody's going to tell my daughter she's crazy."

"But what if I am?" I started to cry. "What if they were right? Mom, I think they were right. All those things they said about depression—I'm so afraid, Mom. I'm so scared that I'm sick—and that you are, too—"

"What are you talking about?" she shrieked.

The car swerved into the left lane, which, mercifully, was empty. She got it back under control, but she was over the edge.

"I am not crazy!" she screamed at me. "Do you hear me? My sister is the crazy one. Not me! And not you, Karen!"

I didn't respond.

I just cried hysterically, and when we got home, I went straight to my room and crawled into bed.

Monday, January 17

I went to every class today and behaved like a model student. Dr. Duffy had said Miss Rand would be told about my situation, but that I didn't have to have sessions with her if I didn't want to. He said he understood if I wanted to keep my personal life separate from school.

So at least I didn't have to deal with her, or O'Neill, right now. I wondered, though, what they and my teachers had been told. I was given take-home tests to make up my grades in every class but art, which was the only one I wasn't failing.

At the end of the day I was walking down the hall toward my locker when I saw Gina and Teddy coming toward me. They were talking and laughing about something, and his hand was on her elbow, kind of steering her through the crowd.

When she saw me, she started to look away.

But our eyes met. I waved at her and forced a smile. I don't know why I did it. But I immediately wished I could take it back, because it would hurt even more when she didn't respond.

For a split second Gina acted shocked. Then she broke into a little smile and waved, too.

That was all. We hurried on in opposite directions.

And I knew that, even though we'd never be best friends again, at least *maybe* Gina didn't hate me.

I was sitting at the desk in my room, taking a geometry test, when my father knocked and came in. He shut the door behind him and said, "Karen, do you have a few minutes? I need to talk to you about something."

"Yeah—sure."

He perched on the edge of my bed. My heart was pounding. I thought at first that he'd found out about what had happened while he was gone. But he didn't seem upset or anything.

"What are you doing?" he asked, peering at the paper and textbook in front of me on my desk.

"Homework."

"Oh, okay. I won't be long."

"It's all right. Is this about the money?" I asked him nervously. "Because I'm not going to go back on our agreement. I'm going to find a job and pay myself back, like we talked about."

He smiled faintly. "I know, Karen. That's not why I wanted to talk to you. Your mother's fortieth birthday is this Thursday."

Relief came over me. "Oh, right."

"So I thought that maybe we'd have a little party for her. Nothing elaborate. Just you and Ethan. I'll take her out for dinner, and then we'll all have cake when we get home."

"Sure."

"Great." He stayed for a few minutes, and we talked about what kind of cake and ice cream to get. Actually, he did most of the talking. I just agreed with everything and told him I'd pick up the cake.

Later, when I was in bed, I started thinking again about what I'd done to myself. Had I really wanted to die?

Death was always something that scared me. But the day I took those pills, I hadn't even been afraid. All I wanted was to escape. I was just trying to get away from the black mood that had been hovering over me.

But I hadn't really wanted to die, had I? Of course not. The thought of it was so terrifying that right then, I was shaking all over.

I hadn't been thinking straight that day.

But what if that happened to me again? What if the black mood came back, and what if this time, no one was there to help me?

20

Thursday, January 20

I went to the bakery after school and picked up the cake my father had ordered for my mother. It was chocolate-raspberry with whipped-cream frosting, and it said "Happy Fortieth Birthday, Sheila" on the top in pink script.

Ethan was home when I got there, and so was my mother. They were both in the kitchen. She was making coffee. Ethan distracted her while I got the cake into my room. My father showed up a little while later to take my mother out to dinner, but she wasn't in the mood. It took a screaming scene to get her out of the house.

"Why is he insisting on this stupid cake and ice cream?" Ethan asked as soon as the door had closed behind them. "She's already a basket case."

My parents pulled into the driveway at eight, and we heard them come into the house, arguing.

Ethan and I were waiting in the kitchen with the cake.

"I don't know why you had to insist that we go to that place, Marty," my mother was saying. "Every single time we go, I order a steak bloody rare, and every time, they bring it to me charred."

"Calm down, Sheila." My father sounded uncomfortable.

"If you were going to take me out on my birthday, why couldn't we have gone to the Capital Grille in Providence? That's my favorite restaurant."

"It was too far away for a week night," my father said, a hint of desperation creeping into his voice. "Come on into the kitchen. I want to show you something."

"No, I don't—"

"Come on, Sheila, it's a present."

"I'm going to bed," my mother said. "I'm tired."

Ethan and I looked at each other, and he rolled his eyes.

My father stood at the bottom of the stairs and called up to my mother, "Sheila?"

My mother only shut the bedroom door.

I looked down at the white candles. The house was completely silent, and the candles started to drip. I blew them out.

Friday, January 21

The sun was shining today, for the first time in weeks. It was warm, too, in the fifties, and the snow and ice were melting. The nice weather made me feel a little surge of hope as I walked home from school. Maybe everything would be all right after all.

But then I thought about last night, and I doubted it.

I'd heard my father come up and knock on the door after Ethan and I had gone to bed. My mother hadn't replied, and when I heard him jiggling the knob, I knew she'd locked herself in.

This morning he'd been lying on the couch downstairs when I got up, still wearing his sweater and rumpled pants. When I went into the kitchen on my way out the door to go to school, he was calling the office and telling them he wouldn't be in because he didn't feel well.

Poor Dad, I thought as I turned the corner onto my street. *Poor Mom. Poor all of us.*

I saw as I got in front of our house that both my parents' cars were in the driveway. I wasn't going to bother to check the mailbox, figuring that one or the other of them would already have done it. But something made me stop and look inside the mailbox anyway, and I saw that it was still full. I flipped through the bills and junk mail as I walked up the driveway, trying to ignore the nagging little feeling in the back of my mind that something was wrong.

But I couldn't ignore it, and it grew, second by second, as I walked around the back of the house. By the time I turned the corner, I knew, somehow, that something was wrong. Terribly, horribly wrong.

And as soon as I saw my father, huddled in his trenchcoat on the bottom step of the deck, as soon as I saw his tear-stained, drawn face, I knew that I was right.

I stopped walking and stared at him for what seemed like minutes, hours. Then I swallowed and asked, "What happened?"

And in the moments before he answered me, the heavy black dread that had been following me for weeks now overtook me. It wrapped itself around me and tried to strangle me, tried to make me stop breathing and black out.

"It's your mother, Karen," my father finally said in a choked voice. "When I woke up at noon, she was still locked in our room, and she wouldn't answer me. I had to break down the door to get in, and . . ." He was crying now, enormous sobs that heaved his entire body.

"No—" was all I could say. "Oh, God." I was backing away from him, a step at a time, my eyes locked on the shattering image of my father crying uncontrollably. "What happened?" I asked. I already knew what he was going to say, but I needed to hear it.

"Karen, she was in the bed, and when I went to her, when I touched her, she was already gone."

"Nooooo!" I screamed.

And then I was running, blindly.

I left my father there, sobbing on the step, and ran away, dropping my books and papers and bag as I ran.

I reached the end of the street and didn't stop, just kept running into the woods, kept running even though branches and twigs slapped me in the face and tangled undergrowth tried to trip me. I kept running through the marshy muck along the creekbed, and then I ran through the creek, the icy, shallow water numbing my feet in my leather boots and taking my breath away.

I ran until I reached the rock Gina and I had guarded from imaginary enemies, the rock that concealed a priceless treasure.

"Karen?"

I looked up. Gina was standing there, looking down at me through the dusky winter air. Her eyes were red and swollen.

"What are you doing here?" I asked woodenly, looking back at the sky. I was lying flat on my back on the hard, cold rock, watching the light fade as the milky winter twilight crept in.

"Ethan told us about—your mother. He said you

had disappeared, and he asked if I had an idea where you might be."

"Oh," I said, watching the sky.

"I didn't know if this was where you'd gone, but I figured maybe . . ."

There were tears in Gina's eyes. She climbed onto the rock next to me, and we stayed there side by side for a long time, not saying anything. Then Gina patted my shoulder. As soon as I felt her touch, I sat up and started to cry.

"It's all right, Karen," she kept saying softly. "It's going to be all right." She hugged me tightly and stroked my hair and I sobbed until I was spent.

Then we walked through the shadowy woods in silence, heading for home.

21

Monday, January 24

The funeral was a blur, just as the past few days had been. Our house was filled with people and food.

Mrs. Petrillo came over to where Gina and I were sitting on folding chairs in the family room. She patted my hand and said, "Karen, I made your favorite peanut butter cookies, the kind with the chocolate chunks. Would you like me to bring you some?"

"No, thanks," I said numbly.

She said something else in a soothing tone, and I nodded vaguely, then watched as she drifted away through the crowd.

I went over the entire scenario in my head once again, as I'd been doing ever since Friday night, when my father had calmly and woodenly told Ethan and me that my mother had killed herself by swallowing pills. Just like I had tried to do. Except that no one found my mother. Not until it was too late.

"Karen?" Gina asked quietly. "Do you want to go up to your room for a while and get away from all these people?"

I looked at her. She didn't look like herself. For one thing, she was wearing black, something Gina never did. And her curls were pulled back into a ponytail. Her complexion was pale, and her eyes were red rimmed.

"No, that's okay," I said dully. I tried to focus on what was going on around me.

I saw Mike and his parents on the couch, talking to Mr. Petrillo and some of the other neighbors. And Ethan was standing in a corner with his friend from the basketball team. He looked stiff in the dark suit my father had bought him.

My father was talking to his brother, my uncle Jimmy, who had flown in on Saturday from North Carolina. My grandma and grandpa Spencer weren't able to travel. Uncle Jimmy said that he'd tried to explain what had happened, but he didn't think they understood.

My mother's parents were here, though. They were in the corner, sitting on folding chairs. My grandfather was being as stoic as he had through the entire ordeal. And my grandmother was crying again as Mrs. Petrillo hovered anxiously around her.

"A lot of people from school were in church, you know?" Gina asked, trying to make conversation.

"Mm-hmm."

Matt had been there. My eyes met his a few times, and what I saw in them was genuine sorrow. And each time I glimpsed it, I hurriedly looked away.

I saw the same expression in Mr. O'Neill's eyes, and in Mrs. Rosenbaum's, and in some of the other teachers'. They all came together in a group. I did my best to avoid all of them, but they took turns coming up to me afterward, saying how sorry they were and hugging me or patting my hand. Miss Rand, I realized now, was the only one who hadn't said not to worry, that everything would be all right. She just gave me a hug and a look that said, *I'm here for you if you need me.*

Thursday, January 27

My grandparents stayed with us all week, insisting on being here "to help." If you asked me, my father and Ethan and I would have been better off on our own, because all my grandmother did was cry, and my grandfather just sat in front of the TV.

Ethan and I spent a lot of time at the movies or just out, walking around. We didn't talk much, and we didn't refer to our mother or what had happened at all.

Now we shuffled home through the January dusk, idly wondering aloud if it was going to snow any more. It had been unseasonably warm all week. You could almost believe spring was around the corner, even though it was still the dead of winter.

When we got home, we took off our coats and hung them on hooks, and heard voices coming from the family room.

"*Told* her she needed to get help when Ethan was a baby and she left him home alone," my father was saying. "But she wouldn't listen to me. She listened to you, Audrey, because you told her she was fine. That it was just postpartum depression or some bull."

"She *was* fine," my grandmother said angrily.

"I always suspected Sheila was manic-depressive, like Jill." He continued to talk, right over my grandmother's protests. "Lately, I've been sure of it. And I know I'm just as guilty as you are of ignoring her behavior. I've been working like a dog lately, and not just because I need the money to pay off the debt Sheila ran up."

Ethan and I looked at each other. I reached out and touched his arm, and we kept listening.

"But you didn't just avoid the problem," my father was saying to my grandmother. "You made her afraid of it. You made her terrified of being 'crazy,' of ending up just like Jill, locked away someplace. For God's sake, you're both so ashamed of your one daughter's illness that now you've destroyed Sheila, too."

My grandmother was crying hysterically. "No, Martin, this is not our fault! Tell him, Hugh. Tell him that we did everything for our girls. We had nothing to do with what happened to them!"

My grandfather only grunted. "Stop that wailing, Audrey."

"I did not destroy my daughters!" my grandmother said, still crying. "They destroyed themselves. *Sheila destroyed herself.*"

"Sheila chose death over admitting that she had a problem, over getting help. She was terrified of how you and Hugh would react. She saw what happened with Jill. You never discuss her. You've rarely visited her in the years she's been at Meadow View."

"That's not true."

"That *is* true," my father said, but I heard his tone softening. "I'm sorry. I know you loved her. I loved her, too. She was my wife," he said hoarsely. "Why didn't I do something?"

My grandmother's sobs died down. I heard footsteps going up the stairs, and realized my father had left the room.

Ethan grabbed his coat again. "I'm going out," he said in a low voice, then fled. I just stood leaning weakly against the wall and hugging myself.

I just realized the truth. About my mother. Not just about what she'd done to herself. But about what she'd done to me.

She'd known I was troubled, and she'd tried to pretend that I was fine. Just like my grandmother, she'd thought that the problems would go away if she didn't acknowledge them—her own problems, and mine, too. She'd never gotten over her parents' shame at the publicity over her sister's suicide attempt, their shame over having a daughter who suffered from a mental illness.

She hadn't wanted to admit that she, like Aunt Jill, was sick.

That she needed help.

Or that I did.

And now it was too late.

Too late for my mother to get help, to save herself.

But it wasn't too late for me.

That night I got a phone call. At first I didn't recognize the voice, but I knew I'd heard it somewhere before.

"Karen? It's Jill. Your aunt Jill."

I didn't know what to say.

"I wanted to call to say how very sorry I was to hear the news. How are you?"

"Okay," I said. Jill sounded so normal. So nice.

"How's your brother?"

"Okay," I said.

Jill explained that my uncle had called her to tell her about my mother. She said she was totally shocked by the news and felt so bad that she hadn't been in touch with my mother for so long.

"I probably wouldn't even recognize you now," she said to me. I found myself trying hard to picture her, but I could only come up with my mother's eyes. It had been eight years since I'd seen her—she must be twenty-eight or -nine now.

She asked me who went to the funeral, and when Ethan and I were going back to school.

She asked me if I would write to her some time. And I said yes. Then she told me she was in a group home and gave me the address.

I thanked her for calling, and then called my father to the phone.

The weirdest thing about the phone call was that Jill sounded so completely normal. Not like the monster everyone made her out to be. Like a perfectly nice person. Not like a crazy lady.

22

Monday, January 31

It was time to go back to school. Time to get on with life.

I got up extra early and took a long, hot shower. Then I carefully dressed in my favorite wool skirt and matching sweater. I put on makeup and jewelry, and I fixed my hair with my blow-dryer and gel to make it smooth, the way my mother had shown me.

My father was sitting at the table, reading the paper and drinking coffee, when I went into the kitchen. "You look pretty, Karen," he said, and he managed a smile, even though his eyes still had that washed-out look. "Going back to school today?"

"Mmm-hmm."

155

"Ethan just left," my father said. "He wanted to get there in time for practice."

I knew my father was going back to work today, too, for the first time. But he'd promised Ethan and me that he'd be home by six and that we'd all have dinner together. My grandmother, before she'd gone home on Saturday, had stocked the freezer with casseroles and soups and stuff. She was trying desperately to help, and my father had thanked her and hugged her.

"Want to have some cereal or something?" my dad asked. He seemed uncomfortable, as though he thought that it was his duty to make sure I ate breakfast.

My mother had never done that, though. And to show him that he didn't have to, either, I said, "It's okay, Dad. I never eat breakfast." I kissed the top of his head.

Outside, the sun was shining as I walked my once familiar path to Gina's house. I hesitated for only a moment before I worked up my nerve and rang the doorbell.

Gina opened the door, surprised to see me. But pleased, too. "Hi, Karen! You going back to school today?"

"Yeah, I thought it was time."

"Want to walk with me?"

"Is it all right? I mean, do you want me to?"

Gina grinned. "Sure! I was getting lonely walking by myself."

She chattered all the way to school, and for that, I was grateful. It was nice just to be with her again, to hear about her and Teddy. He had asked her to the Valentine's Day dance in two weeks, and she told me that her mother had taken her shopping and bought her a new dress.

"You should see it, Karen," she said excitedly. "It's long, kind of like a granny dress, and it has these tiny pink rosebuds splashed all over it. I love it."

"It sounds beautiful," I told her. It was so good to hear her bubbly voice. I could almost pretend that things were back to normal. That everything was the way it used to be.

But deep down, I knew that nothing would ever be the same again.

My mother was gone. Nothing would bring her back. Nothing would change what had happened.

But there was one thing that I *could* change.

When Gina and I got to school, I told her I'd see her and Teddy in the cafeteria. I went to my locker, carefully hung my coat on the hook, and took a deep breath.

Then I walked down the hall to the guidance office. The waiting area was empty. Chewing on my bottom lip, I made myself move forward, until I was standing in the doorway of Miss Rand's office.

She was just sitting down at her desk and she looked up when I knocked on the open door.

"Karen!" she said and beckoned me in.

"Hi."

I hesitated, then took a step inside. And then another.

She was sitting there, watching me.

And waiting.

"Miss Rand?" I said at last. "I think I need help."

23

August 25 . . . Two and a half years later

I stood on the platform, nervously shifting my weight from foot to foot. Next to me, my father was holding my ticket, which he'd made me give him "for safekeeping" before we left the house.

Ethan, who was now taller than my father, was leaning against a pillar, reading *Sports Illustrated* and trying to act as though he wasn't fazed by what was happening. But I knew he was. I knew he'd miss me. So would my dad.

And I'd miss them. I didn't want to think about it, though, or I'd start crying again.

The PA system crackled. "Ladies and gentlemen,

train one fifty-seven to New York City is now arriving on track one."

I could hear it approaching, rumbling along the track, and my stomach did a little flip-flop. I turned to my father and Ethan and thought about how much I hated goodbyes.

Gina and I had had a tearful scene at the airport just last week, before she'd boarded her flight to Washington, D.C., where she was going to Catholic University. She'd been crying for days at the thought of leaving home, even though Teddy, who was at William and Mary, would be nearby. I'd promised to take the Metroliner down to visit her for a weekend as soon as I got settled at F.I.T.

"Well," I said now, as the sound of the train grew closer. "I guess this is it."

"Do you have the emergency credit card I gave you, Karen?" my father asked, and I nodded. It was tucked into my purse, along with the little prescription bottle I'd just had refilled.

Ethan rolled up his magazine, took a few steps forward, and let me hug him. "Don't forget," I said as I squeezed him tightly. "You're coming down on the train to visit on Columbus Day weekend."

He smiled and nodded. "Yeah, cool," he said. "See you."

I swallowed over the lump in my throat and turned to my father. He pulled me close, and I held on to him until I felt a whoosh of air as the train pulled in behind me.

"Make sure to take care of yourself, Karen."

"I will," I said, knowing what he meant. He wanted to make sure I took my pills when I was supposed to—the medication that had made my life bearable again.

Miss Rand had found me a psychiatrist who specialized in teenagers with depression. Dr. Bergstrom was a really nice woman, and after a few sessions I felt pretty comfortable with her. The first session was really hard, though. I couldn't even speak for the first twenty minutes. All I could do was cry. She gave me tissues and told me it was normal to cry. Then she gave me a prescription for an antidepressant. At first we had to adjust the dosage, but it didn't take long before my moods became more even. I didn't feel like crying all the time, and I started sleeping better. And I saw her once or twice a week for the next two and a half years. We talked about everything—my mother, my father, Ethan, school, Matt, Gina. And Jill, too. Dad and Ethan came in for a few sessions, too. Gradually I started doing things again, like drawing. And I got a new job, working in a really cool boutique.

Not that everything was perfect. I still had ups and downs, although nowhere near what they'd been. At least now I usually felt as if I had more control over my life.

In the back of my mind there was always a little bit of fear that those extreme episodes would come back. And even though Dr. Bergstrom assured me that I could always get help when I needed it, I never really felt *entirely* confident.

But I did feel ninety-nine percent better.

I took a deep breath, reached down, and picked up my bag. The rest of my stuff had been sent ahead to my new dorm.

The train ground to a stop, and the conductor stepped off and cheerfully called, "All aboard."

"Well," I said, "I guess I'm off."

I gave a wave and then turned away from my family and climbed up the silver steps into the train.

And as I started down the aisle, looking for a seat, I said silently to my mother, who was always with me, *Look, Mom. I'm on my way.*